Chester
and the
MAGIC 8 BALL

Lynn Katz

Black Rose Writing | Texas

First printing

This is a work of fiction. Names, characters, businesses, places, events, and incidents are either the products of the author's imagination or used in a fictitious manner. Any resemblance to actual persons, living or dead, or actual events is purely coincidental.

ISBN: 978-1-68513-134-0
PUBLISHED BY BLACK ROSE WRITING
www.blackrosewriting.com

Printed in the United States of America
Suggested Retail Price (SRP) $20.95

Chester and the Magic 8 Ball is printed in Bookerly

*As a planet-friendly publisher, Black Rose Writing does its best to eliminate unnecessary waste to reduce paper usage and energy costs, while never compromising the reading experience. As a result, the final word count vs. page count may not meet common expectations.

Cover by Maryia Kapitsa & Kingsize Creations LLC
www.maryia-illustration.com – www.kingsizecreations.com

For Elisha

Chester
and the
MAGIC 8 BALL

Chapter 1
Bored

I turn my Magic 8 Ball around in my hands, warming it up. I don't believe a silly old toy has any more power than a four-leaf clover. But that doesn't stop me.

I might be too old to believe in magic. But like most people, I make a wish right before I blow out my birthday candles and whenever I see a falling star. You never know, right? I shake my Magic 8 Ball a few times and squeeze my eyes tight. I blast my question into the universe like it's a rocket headed for the moon.

"Will I get a dog today?"

I don't just *want* a dog—I *need* a dog. My family *needs* a dog! Any kind of dog will do. A long-haired, yappy, flea-bitten mongrel, a purebred with a smooshed-up face, a dog with short legs and a stubby tail, or even a dog with a runny nose.

There ought to be a law: When you don't have siblings, your parents get a dog. Especially when you've been stuck in a boring house for five boring days of a boring February vacation. Especially when the weather is miserable and your best friend, Emma, is skiing with her family in Vermont. If I had a dog, I wouldn't be bored and I wouldn't be lonely, and maybe my parents would stop arguing. Dogs are even more magical than blowing out birthday candles on your cake, more magical than this silly toy.

Uncle Doug gave me a Magic 8 Ball for my birthday when I was at that *asking-too-many-questions* stage. After that birthday, whenever I asked a question, Uncle Doug would say, "Don't ask me, Georgia, ask the Magic 8 Ball." I can't always count on this shiny black ball with the big white number. It doesn't always give me the answers I want, but it's only wrong about fifty percent of the time. And when I don't like the answer, I try again.

I whisper my question louder this time, in case the Magic 8 Ball that I don't believe is magical didn't hear me. "Will I get a dog today?"

I open my eyes, turn the ball so the window is facing me, and wait for the message to rise to the surface. The answers I get are sometimes clear and sometimes murky. Like the dark blue, inky liquid they're floating in. What will the answer be today?

Most likely? Ask again later? Signs point to yes? Don't count on it? Very doubtful?

When I peer into the small window, I can't believe the words I'm seeing. *It is certain.* I blink. I squint. *It is certain?* On the very first try! Usually it takes two or three tries to get anything close to certainty.

I scrunch my eyes closed, open them, and look again. The words haven't changed: *It is certain.* It is certain I will get a dog. TODAY! I want to believe it. I *need* to believe it. I pump my fist into the air. YES! My scalp tingles, and my heart flutters. Maybe I'm on a lucky streak. And so, I ask my second important question of the day:

"Will my parents stop arguing?"

I should quit while I'm ahead. I should be happy with the positive answer about getting a dog. But I'm greedy. The words float up to the surface: *It is doubtful.* I refuse to let this negative prediction destroy my good mood. Besides, once we get our dog, my parents will be happy and our family will be complete.

Although encouraged by my Magic 8 Ball's certainty about getting a dog, I need a plan. Somehow, I need to get my mom to drive us to the Humane Society where we will find the perfect dog. Big problem: she hates driving in bad weather. I need to be persuasive.

Persuasive Idea Number 1: BOREDOM

I find my mom in the hallway, organizing the linen closet for the third time this week. "I'm bored!" I say. I plop down inches away from where she's sitting on the floor. "It's February vacation. Kids are not supposed to be bored during their vacations." My mom is working extra hard to ignore me. Ignoring kids is her superpower. Which is surprising, given her career choice is teaching high school.

"Work through it, Georgia," she says, folding a peach-colored washcloth as though she's working on an origami project. "A little boredom builds character. Trust me, boredom is a passage to creative thinking."

"I say boredom is a passage to misery. Let's go somewhere," I beg. "Anywhere!" Now she's tilting her head to the side, studying the stacks of hand and bath towels, rearranging them like she's an artist creating a sculpture for the Museum of Modern Art. It's time to try Persuasive Idea Number 2.

Persuasive Idea Number 2: DAD'S A BETTER PARENT

"I wish Dad were home. *He'd* take me someplace cool. You never take me anywhere!" My mom continues to ignore me, and now she's singing some old rock and roll song about how you can't always get what you want.

This *Dad's a better parent* idea isn't working either. I storm away, leaving her sprawled on the floor surrounded by her piles of precious towels. I slam my bedroom door with just enough force to get my message across, but not so much force that I get myself in trouble.

I need a better strategy. The first step to getting a dog today is convincing my mom to leave the house. All this week the roads have been icier than usual, so persuading her to drive will be a challenge. I turn to my Magic 8 Ball again. "Hmm. Will my mom take me out for lunch today?" I roll the ball around the floor, and it stops at my pile of laundry in the corner of the room. Yes, my room's a mess, but no, unlike my mom, I'm never in the mood to organize anything.

I scoop up the Magic 8 Ball and read the answer: *It is decidedly so.* That's all the encouragement I need. I run down the hall, ready to present my third persuasive idea.

Persuasive Idea Number 3: IT'S JUST LUNCH

"Mom, guess what, we're going out to lunch," I tell her, showing her the Magic 8 Ball answer. "You can't argue with my Magic 8 Ball." Before she has time to prove me wrong, her phone rings.

"Argh! I left my phone in the kitchen. Could you grab it for me, Georgia?" I place my Magic 8 Ball on the floor where my mom can read the message in the window, and I run to the kitchen. I grab the phone from the counter on the third ring. It's my dad.

"Hey, Georgia. Listen, it's going to be a late night again. Big car accident on the highway. Multiple vehicles. Lots of injuries. And the hospital is short-staffed." My dad's a trauma nurse in a giant hospital. He works in the emergency room. "You two should have dinner without me. Tell Mom not to wait up."

"I'll tell her, Dad," I say. "We miss you."

"Gotta go. Love you," he says.

I drag my feet back to the linen closet, where my mom's still humming and doing her organizing thing. I'm about to ruin her day. "Dad's going to be late again. Car accident. He says we should have dinner without him." I'm leaning against the wall, keeping my distance, waiting for the explosion. My mom looks up at me with wide, watery eyes. She seems more disappointed than angry this time. She sighs and shakes her head.

"The third time this week." My mom hates it when Dad has to stay late at work. That's one of the reasons they've been arguing so much lately.

She's sitting there on the floor looking miserable, surrounded by washcloths, wearing an old purple scrunchie to keep her straggly hair out of her face, and I can't help but feel sorry for her. She needs to get out of the house as much as I do. "We're going out to lunch, right?" I'm pointing to the Magic 8 Ball. "It'll do us both good." And then, she looks up at me again, and she says the magic words I want to hear.

"Fine, Georgia. You're impossible. Let me finish organizing the linen closet, and I'll take you out for lunch. But I'm choosing the restaurant, and I'm in the mood for Chinese food."

"Yippee!" Mission accomplished. And lucky for me, I didn't need to use Persuasive Idea Number 4, which would involve bribing my mom and then having to spend the rest of my vacation cleaning up the mess in my bedroom. Of course, Persuasive Idea Number 4 might come in handy *after* lunch when I need to convince her to visit the Humane Society.

Chapter 2
Goldfish

Finally, the linen closet is ridiculously organized, and my mom is ready. The purple scrunchie is gone, and she's changed out of my dad's old T-shirt and sweatpants from the last century. Now she's wearing one of her teacher outfits, and she looks ready for a lunch date with her daughter. "Let's go," she says.

I grab my Magic 8 Ball and slip it into my backpack. It may come in handy later. We spend ten hours scraping the ice off the car windows, and my hands are freezing inside my mittens. I think about the dog that might be joining our family, and that thought warms my heart. Today is the day! *It is certain.* Nothing else matters.

The roads are slick, and my mom's driving fifteen miles an hour. Not too many cars are on the roads. Mom's knuckles are white, clutching the wheel as though she's steering the Titanic and trying to avoid an iceberg. I've pulled my long hair over my shoulder, and I'm braiding and unbraiding it, which is something I do when I feel jittery. It helps calm me down. Mom hates when I do that.

"Stop braiding your hair. You're making me even more nervous," my mom says. Except for the length of our hair, I look a lot like my mom. Maybe it's the shape of our faces, the bangs, the light brown hair, which for me reaches my waist and for my mom hits her shoulders. Of course, she has the straightest teeth in the universe, and one day I'll have those straight teeth, too, if I ever lose the braces.

I toss my halfway-braided hair behind my shoulder. The last thing I want to do is make my mom more nervous, but now that I've convinced her to leave the house, it's time for PART II of my plan. I pull out my Magic 8 Ball. I ask the question loud enough for my mom to hear, but not so loud she's distracted. "So, Magic 8 Ball, will we visit the Humane Society after lunch?" My mom's laughing. She thinks I'm funny, which is not necessarily a bad thing.

Begging my parents for a dog is an ongoing theme in our household. Every birthday. Every Christmas. Every time I get a good report card. Unfortunately, my parents and Santa have never agreed to let me get a *real* pet.

No dogs for our family. My parents have their reasons, although they are not, in my opinion, particularly good reasons: "Dogs cost too much money," my dad says. "Dogs make a mess, and we're too busy to take care of a dog," my mom says.

The main reason, the reason they like to hold over my head, has more to do with trust. They don't trust their only child to take care of a pet. But today might be different. Today might be the day! If you can believe a Magic 8 Ball.

"Mom, my Magic 8 Ball says *Ask again later*. I'll ask again after lunch."

"Georgia, can't you see I'm trying to concentrate on my driving?" my mom says. "And don't bother asking again. We will *not* be going to the Humane Society."

"But, Mom, you can't argue with the Magic 8 Ball!"

"Oh yes I can. There is no way we're going to visit those mangy, vicious, growling canines behind cages. Unless of course your Magic 8 Ball wants to do the driving." *Ha ha ha.* Not at all funny.

"Mom, we wouldn't be adopting a dog at the Humane Society. We'd just be looking. Think of it as going to the movies. It's something fun to do."

"We're going out to lunch. That's something fun to do. And, Georgia, remember the goldfish."

The goldfish. It's always about the goldfish. Suddenly, my faith in the Magic 8 Ball's *It is certain* answer evaporates. I need to face the truth about my lonely only-child life. I'll never get a dog. No canine bestie, no one to hang out with after school. No one to listen to me and play with me and love me no matter what. Who am I kidding? Three little words, *remember the goldfish*, tell me everything I need to know.

Chapter 3
Fortune Cookies

The first thing I notice when I walk through the door of Chengdu Gardens is the aquarium in the middle of the restaurant. *Ugh.* The universe is plotting against me. *Remember the goldfish.* How could I forget?

When I was six years old, my parents gave me the goldfish test. It's simple. When your child starts nagging you for a pet, you buy a goldfish and wait for the goldfish to die. Then, when the goldfish dies, you shrug your shoulders and tell your child, *"If you can't even keep an itty-bitty goldfish alive, there is no way we're going to get you a dog."* My parents went all out and bought two goldfish. I named them Fish One and Fish Two. Fish One died in three days. Fish Two jumped out of his bowl the next night, probably because he went looking for his pal, Fish One. Any way you look at it—I failed the goldfish test. And my parents won't let me forget it.

Chengdu Gardens is always packed, and today is no exception. The spicy smell of ginger, garlic, and sesame makes my mouth water. As we walk to our table, I think about trying to block my mom's view of the aquarium, but it's too late. She points and says, "Speaking of goldfish..."

Mom perks up as we devour our steamed dumplings and Sichuan chili chicken. The food's spicy, making my eyes water. I want to keep Mom happy, so I let her share her latest teacher stories without interrupting her.

"So, you'll love this one, Georgia," she tells me. She dips the last dumpling into a small dish of soy sauce. It takes forever when she's trying to tell a story and eat at the same time. "One of my tenth-grade students claimed he couldn't concentrate on his homework." She stuffs the dumpling into her mouth. I wait. She chews. I wait. She swallows. "And you won't believe his excuse. He can't concentrate because the dishwasher's too loud."

My mom is not the least bit sympathetic when it comes to lame excuses like noisy kitchen appliances. I usually love my parents' work stories, but now all I can think about is the dog I plan to meet at the Humane Society. My hopes are dangerously high, but I can't help myself.

"Mom. Do your students ever tell you their dogs ate their homework?" My mom sees right through my phony question.

"Georgia, don't start begging for a dog again." I cup my hand behind my ear, pretending I can't hear her. It's noisy in the restaurant, what with all the people chattering away and the clattering of dishes every time the kitchen door opens.

I scrunch my face like I'm confused. "What's that? What did you say? You want me to ask the Magic 8 Ball again? Sure!" I sneak my hand into the backpack sitting on the bench next to me, and I pull out my Magic 8 Ball. "Should we go to the Humane Society today? Asking for a friend," I say.

"I don't care what your Magic 8 Ball tells you. We're not going."

I look down at the answer. "Mom, look—the answer is *It is certain.* And besides, Dad's coming home late tonight. We have the whole afternoon. The linen closet is perfect, there's nothing else to do."

Before my mom can argue with me, our waiter brings the check and a plate of orange and pineapple slices.

"Thank you. Everything was delicious, as usual," my mom says.

The waiter glances down at the table. "Ah, I see you have a Magic 8 Ball. My daughter has one, too. There's no need for magic here at Chengdu Gardens. We have our lucky goldfish."

"Lucky goldfish?" I ask.

"Goldfish are very lucky. They symbolize a long life." Our waiter points to the line of customers waiting for a table. "And as you can see, they've made our restaurant very busy. Sometimes too busy."

"Long life? Really?" my mom snickers. "My daughter had goldfish, but she couldn't keep them alive for even a week." My face burns. I glare at my mom, letting her know it is not okay to share this embarrassing information with the world.

"You need a bigger tank. Not a small fishbowl. If you treat the goldfish right, they'll live a long time and give you luck." I look at my mom again. But this time, I'm the one snickering. My parents can't use the goldfish test against me anymore. I now have something to hold over *their* heads. They were the ones who bought a tank that was too small for those doomed goldfish.

The waiter leaves us with two fortune cookies. I open the first one and pretend to read the words on the thin slip of paper. "It says, '*You and your mom will fall in love with a dog today.*'"

My mom doesn't believe me, of course. "Let me see that." She grabs the fortune out of my hand.

"Actually, it says, '*If you throw mud, you lose ground,*'" she reads. "Really, Georgia, you are too much. You never give up, do you?" Then she unwraps her own cookie and breaks it apart, pulling out the fortune. "Oh, nice," she says. She pretends to read the words. "You'll love this, Georgia. It says, '*Your daughter will clean her bedroom, fold her laundry, and stop nagging you for a dog.*'" I grab the slip of paper out of her hand.

"As a matter of fact, it says, '*All things are difficult before they are easy*.' Maybe having a daughter with a messy room will be easy for you one day!"

We're laughing about the fortunes and the goldfish test as we trudge back to the car. As we wait for the defroster to clear the front and back windshields, my Magic 8 Ball is warming up in my hands. That's when I decide to try Persuasive Idea Number 4. What have I got to lose?

Persuasive Idea Number 4: BRIBERY

"Mom, now that we know it wasn't *my* fault the goldfish died, can we go to the Humane Society if I promise to clean my bedroom tomorrow?"

"Does that promise include your closet?"

"Yup!"

"Your laundry?"

"Yup!"

"You'll make your bed?"

"I'll even make my bed."

"Oh, Georgia. I give up," Mom says. "You win. But remember, we're just looking!"

"I know. I know—we're just looking," I say. *Never underestimate the power of a bribe*, I think as I place my Magic 8 Ball in my backpack.

Chapter 4
Just Looking

Back on the icy roads, I'm braiding and unbraiding my hair again, and my mom's knuckles are bloodless. Finally, we skid into the parking lot of the Humane Society. "We made it, Mom!" I cheer her on.

"Georgia—I can't believe I let you talk me into driving here on those slippery roads. It's a miracle we didn't end up in Dad's emergency room."

I bounce down the shoveled walkway, ten paces ahead of her, as I make my way into the building. The lobby smells more like a flower shop than an animal shelter. My mom catches up with me, and we stand at the main desk, waiting for someone to tell us what to do. Finally, a woman points to the written directions on a clipboard. She doesn't even look up from her computer. I'm hoping the dogs are friendlier than the humans.

We need to fill out a million forms before we're allowed to look at any of the animals. I pace the waiting room floor while my mom deals with the paperwork. She can't stop complaining. "I don't know why we have to answer all these questions. We're just looking." *We're just looking. Bet the people who work here have heard that phrase a few billion times,* I think.

I pull out my Magic 8 Ball while my mom is busy with paperwork. "Will I find a dog to adopt today?" I whisper. I shake the ball and turn it around. I wait for the answer to appear. I'm feeling more optimistic than ever before. Maybe it's the goldfish. Maybe it's the message on my mom's fortune cookie. *All things are difficult before they are easy.* My family's ready for easy. And maybe, it's something in the way my mom is acting, as though she's softening. Maybe she's lonely, too, and a dog is what we both need. I look down at the message in the Magic 8 Ball's window, and I'm not disappointed. *It is certain.*

Finally, the woman at the counter directs us to the dog adoption area. The room is enormous. We stroll up and down rows of wire kennels. It smells like what you'd expect with so many canines in one huge space. I don't mind the doggy smell one bit. A few of the dogs are barking, trying to get our attention.

Here's the first thing my mom notices: "Check out the names," she says. "Dog naming must be a lost art." She's right. Most of the female dogs have cute human names: Chloe, Gracie, Lucy, Hazel, and Winifred. The male dogs have the more ridiculous names related to the way they look or their personalities: Sandy, Pepper, Fatness, Chewie, Mr. Pooh-Pooh.

"Who would adopt a dog named Mr. Pooh-Pooh?" I ask. We're both giggling now as we stroll down the next row of kennels.

"What kind of person names a dog Sniper? Or worse—Dawg the Dog? Really? That's the best they could come up with?" Mom asks. I'm cracking up, because I'm looking at Dawg the Dog, and he doesn't even look like a dog. He looks more like a teddy bear. I clutch my stomach and snort, which happens sometimes when I laugh too hard.

"Georgia, quiet down. We're going to get kicked out of here!" But then Mom makes me laugh even harder, because here's the second thing she notices:

"There are way too many pit bull mixes here." She's right. The Humane Society is teeming with those mutts. It seems pit bulls like to make puppies with every other breed imaginable. Pit bull and Rottweiler mix, pit bull and Doberman mix, pit bull and boxer mix, pit bull and terrier mix.

"Hey, where's the pit bull and pit bull mix? I want one of those." We're both giggling as we make our way down the next row.

I take my time, gazing into each cage. My heart's filled with hope. I'm trying desperately to fall in love with a dog, any dog. I don't care about their names or their breed. I need a dog to love, to play with, a dog who will listen to me, and hang out with me, and maybe a dog who will stop my parents from arguing so much and bring us all together. One big happy family. That's not asking for too much. But how will I know when I meet "the one?" How does anyone know when they fall in love?

I stop at the cage of a yellow lab mix. She seems gentle and sweet, curled up on her cushion. Her name is Cutie-Pie, which isn't the name I would choose, but I don't care. I reach into the cage with my right hand, palm lifted. Cutie-Pie walks over. She sniffs my hand and looks up with a furrowed brow and sad eyes, as though she's saying, "Take me, take me, please take me home with you."

"What do you think, Mom?" She's several cages ahead of me but walks back to check out Cutie-Pie.

"Too old," she says. "You need to read their bios, Georgia." She points to the display frames hanging on the wire cages. Each frame includes information about the animal waiting for adoption—their age, breed, and a paragraph about what each pet is looking for. Cutie-Pie is almost my age. And in dog years, she's a senior citizen. "Older dogs can have health problems," my mom says. "Expensive vet bills. We can't afford that. Besides, we're just looking," she reminds me. Or maybe she's reminding herself. *Poor Cutie-Pie.*

I stop outside another cage. This dog is a terrier mix. His name is Sparky, and he's only four years old. He's barking wildly and practically doing somersaults when I stop to say hello. He's so happy to have attention. "Mom, check out little Sparky! He's adorable!" She studies the information posted about Sparky and starts reading aloud.

"Sparky wants a big yard for lots of exercise." Then she whispers, "Absolutely not. 'Wants a big yard' is Humane Society code for wild and uncontrollable. Besides, Georgia, we are just looking." *Poor little Sparky.*

As we reach the last row of cages, one beagle mix snarls at us when we move too close to his cage. I jump away. "Not a great way to impress a potential parent!" I say. And besides, naming a dog Barky is horrible advertising.

"That does it. I'm done," my mom says. "Let's get out of here. This place is putting me in a grumpy mood."

I'm feeling grumpy, too, but not because of the place. I mean the dogs are all clean, not at all mangy as my mom expected. And despite their silly names, they seem to be healthy and well-cared for, and every single one has a comfy blanket and toys. I'm grumpy because I haven't found *the one*. I haven't found the one dog who will be coming home with us. I haven't found the dog who will work its magic for our family.

I'm dragging my feet. "Can't we look one more time?" I ask.

"No, Georgia. I'm worried about the drive home on those icy roads."

My heart breaks for all those poor homeless dogs in their lonely cages. I wanted to fall in love. Finding a dog today was supposed to be certain. I should never have trusted my Magic 8 Ball.

Chapter 5
Chester

As we walk to the front desk to sign out, I notice a photograph on the bulletin board. It's a picture of a sandy-colored dog with deep, dark eyes. The dog's pink tongue is sticking out from the corner of his mouth. The notice reads: *Interested in meeting Chester? Chester is an adult Schnoodle-mix who needs a loving home. Ask at the front desk.* Hmm. A loving home, we could manage that. I wonder why they didn't keep Chester in one of the cages with the other dogs.

"Mom, check out Chester," I say, pointing to the picture. "He's so cute, isn't he?"

"I'm done looking, Georgia. We're going home," my mom says, not even glancing at the photograph of Chester. Her cell phone rings, and while she's answering it, I walk up to the front desk.

"Can I help you?" The guy behind the counter is wearing a tag with his name scribbled in bad second-grade handwriting. I can barely read it. I think it says Mr. Ryan. He looks like a high school kid with a volunteer job to keep him busy during vacation week.

"We'd like to meet Chester, the dog in the picture," I say.

"Ah, Chester's a sweetie." I wish the woman who ignored us before would wait on me. I don't think Mr. Ryan knows what he's doing. But he's the only person at the counter, and I have questions that need answers before my mom gets off the phone and drags me out of here.

"What's a Schnoodle? Is that a pit bull mix? And if he's such a sweetie, why isn't he with the other dogs?" Sometimes I blurt out whatever's on my mind. My mom says I need to stop and think, count to ten. Who has time to count to ten? I can barely speed count to three before the words fly off my tongue.

"A Schnoodle is part schnauzer and part poodle. There may be some other breeds in Chester, too." Mr. Ryan grabs a keyring from under the counter. "He came back from the hospital yesterday. Chester had to have all his teeth removed, but he's doing well."

My mom's clutching her cell phone as she joins me at the counter. She's scowling, and her hands are on her hips. She's probably furious I'm wasting more time at the Humane Society.

"A toothless dog?" my mom scoffs, curling her lip.

"Why did he have to have all his teeth removed?" I ask.

"Chester's former guardian didn't take care of his teeth these past few years. She was in her nineties and had to move into an assisted-living apartment. She couldn't keep him. Don't get me wrong, she gave him lots of love and attention but maybe too many sweets. Very bad idea. Most of Chester's teeth were decayed."

My mom jumps in with questions of her own. "How old is Chester? And how's he supposed to eat with no teeth?" I like that my mom is asking questions. I like that she's using Chester's name.

"Not sure about Chester's age. We think he's around five years old, despite the condition of his teeth. He's been eating soft food, and he's ready to handle a kibble diet. His gums will toughen up. But I'm going to warn you, if you meet him, you will fall in love." I'm waiting for my mom to say she's not interested. I'm waiting for her to complain about the drive home and the icy roads. And then she surprises me.

"I guess it wouldn't hurt to meet him," she says, shrugging her shoulders.

"Follow me." Mr. Ryan saunters down a short hallway, his keys jingling. He unlocks the door of a small meeting room for potential adoptees. "Wait here. It will only take a minute," he says, closing the door behind him.

I can't sit still, and I'm practically jumping up and down. I'm also braiding and unbraiding my hair so my hands will have something to do.

"Stop it, Georgia. You're making me nervous," my mom says.

"I can't help it, I'm too excited!" And then to make conversation, I ask, "Who called before?"

"It was your dad. He's not coming home tonight."

"What? Why?" I can't remember the last time he worked a double-shift.

"He said it's going to be an all-nighter, lots of broken bones, emergency surgeries. He won't be home until tomorrow morning." I know that look on my mom's face when she's ready to explode. Her lower lip juts out a mile, and she crosses her arms over her chest. I want to say something to make her feel better, but as usual, I say the wrong thing.

"Don't be mad, Mom. He's saving lives, it's important work. It's not Dad's fault."

"We're important too, Georgia. His family should be as important as his job." I know she's proud of my dad being a trauma nurse. But I understand she gets lonely, especially when he works long hours.

Suddenly, my mom looks up, and I follow her gaze. Mr. Ryan's face is in the window. The door opens, and Chester, a twenty-five-pound toothless bundle of joy, leaps into the room. He goes right to my mom as though I don't exist. He puts his adorable head on her knee and looks up into her face. She starts smoothing the soft fur between his ears. It's hard to keep my distance, but I've waited this long, and I can wait a little longer. Right now, it's my mom and Chester who need to fall in love.

"Hello, Chester. Hello, boy," my mom says. When she stops petting him, Chester lays his paw on her arm, as if to say "More, please!"

"Oh my, aren't you a sweetie," she says. "You know what you want, don't you, Chester?" Then Chester rolls over onto his back, and I think he smiles at me. I join my mom and start rubbing his belly. His fur is so soft and shiny clean, the color of bleached sand. His little pink tongue is peaking out of the corner of his mouth, and his tail is wagging a hundred miles an hour. Chester even smells yummy. I think he had a strawberry scented bubble bath.

Sometimes you know in your gut when something is true. Sometimes you are one hundred percent sure. And I know Chester's perfect. I know Chester is exactly what we've waited for. After loving him up and watching my mom melt right before my eyes like an ice cube in the summer sun, I do what I have to do to make this happen for my family. I'm down on my knees next to Chester. I look up at my mom, and I promise her the moon.

I promise I will walk Chester at least twice a day.

I promise I will clean up all his messes in the house, if he makes any messes, which I am sure he won't because…

I promise to train him to do his business outside, and…

I promise to be a good citizen and not leave his poop on people's property when I walk him outside.

I promise to keep his food and water bowls clean.

I promise to work hard in school and get amazing report cards to hang on the refrigerator door.

I promise to stop leaving my dirty clothes on the floor of my bedroom.

I promise to fold the towels into thirds so they'll all fit in the linen closet.

I promise I will never ask for anything ever again as long as I live.

I promise to write flowery essays about what an amazing mother I have for the yearly Mother's Day essay contest in the Hartford Courant.

I think that last promise is what tilts the results in my favor. *Signs point to YES.* And my mom says, "Georgia, I think Chester's the one. What do you think?" Tears are streaming down her face. Chester barks twice and wags his tail. I put my arms around my mom. And for the first time in my life, I truly understand what people mean when they talk about tears of joy.

Chapter 6
Last Straw

I'm sitting in the back seat with Chester, his adorable snout on my knee. We're driving to the pet store to buy food and supplies. "Dad will be okay with Chester, right, Mom? Should we call him?"

My mom tries to reassure me. "He'll be fine. With your dad working late hours all the time, he's almost never home. He won't have to take care of Chester. It won't be his problem, so it shouldn't be his decision. Besides, what's done is done." I'm not convinced, but my mom seems happy, and I'm so over the moon about Chester I let it go. Life is perfect for the next sixteen hours. My heart is overflowing with love for Chester. I can't wait for Emma to return from her ski trip. She's going to flip when she meets him.

When we finally get home, Mom unpacks the dog food and equipment while I give Chester a tour. He sniffs every piece of furniture, my dad's slippers next to my parents' bed, the pile of dirty clothes in the corner of my bedroom, the trash can in the kitchen. He keeps looking up at me as if to say, "Am I dreaming? Is this really my new home?" Mom pours kibble into his bowl, and we watch him practically inhale his dinner. I'm sitting on the floor a few feet away from Chester as he eats, and I could watch him all day.

"Mom, this is better than TV!" She's watching Chester, too, as he laps up water and then wipes his face with his paws. Finally, he trots over to me and snuggles into my lap to cuddle. Every single thing that dog does is adorable.

"Mom, get your cell phone and take a picture of Chester on my lap so I can text it to Emma." I put my head close to Chester's and grin like I won the lottery, which, in a way, I did. I text my best friend.

Georgia: Check out the newest member of our family!
Emma: WHAT???
Georgia: His name's Chester
Emma: OMG OMG OMG
Georgia: Can't wait for you to get home and meet him
Emma: OMG OMG OMG he's so cute I'm in love

"Mom, Emma says she's in love with Chester. Should we send the picture to Dad?" I ask.

"Absolutely not. He's busy at the hospital. He'll find out when he comes home tomorrow morning." I'm getting more nervous about my dad's reaction, but deep down I'm thinking, *Who could resist this amazing dog?*

That night my mom makes Chester sleep in his new crate. We set it up in the kitchen and put his Humane Society blanket in there. I even toss in an old stuffed animal my parents gave me for Christmas years ago. It's a pink puppy with yellow polka dots all over it. I loved that stuffed puppy, and I named it Dottie. But when I figured out Dottie was supposed to make me forget about wanting a real dog, I lost interest. I'm thinking Dottie still smells like me, and that will help Chester feel safe.

Chester doesn't mind going into his crate, but once he realizes we aren't staying with him, I worry he'll have a change of heart. We keep the oven light on so it won't be too dark in the kitchen. Then we leave Chester all alone with only Dottie and his blanket to keep him company.

Of course, I can't sleep, partly because I'm excited and partly because I can hear the sound of Chester whimpering. My heart's breaking for poor Chester, all alone in a strange place, with no one to comfort him.

Finally, I can't take it anymore. I bring my pillow and blanket to the kitchen and curl up on the floor right next to the crate. "Don't worry, Chester.

You're not alone. I'm right here with you," I say. He stops whimpering as soon as he hears my voice. I squeeze my hand through the bars of his crate, and he puts his paw right into my palm. Soon Chester's eyes close, and his entire body exhales. The sound of Chester's breathing makes me smile. Paw in hand, I watch him sleep for a while. And then, before I know it, it's morning, and my mom's waking me up.

"Georgia, wake up, honey." I open my eyes. My body aches from sleeping on the hard kitchen floor. My mom lets Chester out of his cage. He jumps all over me, his tongue laps my face, and he trots around the kitchen like it's Christmas morning. "I'll take Chester out," my mom says. "You get this pillow and blanket out of the kitchen before your dad gets home."

To say my dad's *surprised* when he walks in the front door at 9:15 a.m. seeing his wife, his daughter, and a toothless dog sitting on the couch as though the dog lives there—which, in fact, he does—would be the understatement of the century. Surprised doesn't even come close to describing my dad's reaction. Shocked? Closer. Astonished, flabbergasted, stunned, speechless? Closer, but in fact, there is no word to describe the look on my dad's face.

My mom is sipping a cup of tea. She waits. She watches. I'm rubbing Chester behind his floppy ears. I study my dad's face. I expect he'll fall in love with Chester exactly like we did. I mean, who wouldn't love this sweet boy? Chester is wagging his tail. He waits. He watches. And then my dad begins to speak, and my heart begins to sink.

"What... the heck... is that?" he asks my mom. He doesn't even take off his heavy winter coat. His voice is quiet and low, mournful, and you can almost see steam coming out of his ears. "Why... is there... a dog... on... our... couch?"

"I can explain," I say, but my dad interrupts.

"Georgia... go... to... your... room." He points his finger in the direction of my bedroom.

"Can I take Chester with me?"

Suddenly, everything speeds up. This train is moving way too fast. "Georgia, go to your room. NOW!"

My dad doesn't raise his voice often, but when he does, things are serious. I run to my room without Chester, but the yelling continues. I press my ear to the door, and I hear bits and pieces, words and phrases, crying and sobbing that go on and on for a very long time.

I get the gist of my parents' fight. And poor Chester, who has to sit right in the middle of it, must be getting the gist, too.

You know we can't afford... You know how much Georgia wants... I don't care what you say... This is the last straw... You're always working late... You

*should have called me... You never would have
agreed... You're being unreasonable... You went
behind my back... You're never even home... It's
either me or the dog... His name is Chester...
Remember the goldfish... I can't do this anymore...
I'm done... Then go...*

Finally, I hear a loud thud that can only be the
sound of our front door. A few seconds later, my
parents' bedroom door slams so hard my mom's
teacup collection rattles in the dining room hutch.

I'm shaking all over like those teacups, and tears
are streaming down my face. Yesterday was the
happiest day of my life. Yesterday was magical. I
finally got what I wanted. The sweetest dog, a
dream come true, a best friend. Life was perfect an
hour ago, and now... now... my world has come
crashing down like a huge wave smashing me
under the water. I can barely stand up. I can barely
breathe.

I shuffle into the bathroom and splash cold
water all over my face. Everything is different now.
I have Chester to think about. I have to put my own
sadness, my own needs to the side. He's counting on
me.

I tiptoe into the living room. Chester's still
sitting on the couch. He's not wagging his tail
anymore. He looks lost, and he's whimpering. Poor
Chester. He doesn't deserve this. I start to cry again,
but I wipe my eyes with the back of my hand and

bury my face in Chester's fur to muffle the sound of my sobbing. Finally, I pull myself together, because no matter what else is going on, Chester needs me.

I run to the kitchen to grab one of the biodegradable pooper-scooper bags we bought at the pet store and the leash they gave us at the Humane Society. Chester stays at my side, like a shadow. I need to prove I can take care of him. At the very least, I can keep the living room rug poop-free and keep Chester healthy, unlike those poor goldfish.

"Let's go, Chester. Time to get to know your new neighborhood." That's all it takes to put Chester in a good mood. He wags his tail and looks up at me as though I'm his best friend in the world.

I'm walking Chester around the block, avoiding patches of sidewalk ice. The sun is shining, turning the roads to slush. Chester marks his territory, painting patches of crunchy snow a pale shade of yellow. Despite the sunshine, I can see my breath in the cold air, and I'm glad Chester has a fluffy coat to keep him warm.

I'm trying not to worry. I remind myself that my family has been here before. This is not the first time my dad has walked out the door in an angry huff. This is hardly the first argument they've had, and I'm sure it won't be the last.

I can't remember a time my parents could get through a day without arguing about something.

My mom yells at my dad for leaving the lights on all over the house and blames him for our high electricity bills. My dad yells at my mom for wasting money on expensive brands of laundry detergent instead of buying the cheaper store brands. My mom gets mad at my dad because he never does the laundry so why should he decide their brand of detergent! My dad gets mad at my mom because he's tried to do the laundry but my mom is never happy about the way he folds the towels. They fight, and then they make up. Why should this argument be any different?

By the time we make it home, I've talked myself into feeling more optimistic. "Everything is going to be fine, Chester. You'll see. The outlook is good for your new family."

Chapter 7
Eavesdropping

Going back to school after February vacation isn't easy. I worry about Chester spending his days in the crate all by himself. But my mom says Chester needs his sleep and that's what he'll do while we're at school.

One week later, we've worked out a schedule. My mom walks Chester first thing in the morning because she's out of bed before I open my eyes. I'm in charge of feeding him breakfast and dinner, and I wash his bowls every day. My mom gets home before I do in the afternoon, so she walks him and plays with Chester before she makes dinner. When I get home, I give him another walk and play for a while outside to make sure he gets enough exercise. He keeps me company while I'm doing homework. Then together, we give him one final walk before bedtime.

I haven't told anyone about my dad moving out. Not even Emma. Telling my best friend would make it too real, too permanent, and I know he'll be back.

It's Friday night, and Emma and I are sitting at our kitchen table, stuffing our faces with my mom's almost-world-famous lasagna. Chester's curled up near my feet. Emma doesn't notice my dad's not around. She assumes he's working late, as usual. Emma says, "You have the perfect dog. He doesn't even beg for food, and he's so cute and well-behaved. You're so lucky!"

"I know. It's weird he's only been with us for a few weeks, but he's already part of our family. I can't imagine not having Chester in my life," I say.

"Wish my parents would get *me* a dog," Emma says. We both know that will never happen because her little brother has allergies.

After dinner, Emma and I are hanging out in my bedroom, finishing our math homework. We take a break to play tug of war with Chester using one of my mom's old socks. Even though we let him win, for a toothless dog, Chester has strong jaws.

And then we begin talking about school and our favorite classes. My favorite class is math. I like that there are right answers and wrong answers—no hazy answers. Emma's taking Chinese so she can communicate with her grandparents in their first language. That's her favorite class. And then, in the middle of our conversation about school, Emma brings up my least favorite person in the universe: Reagan Worthington.

"You know," Emma says. "Reagan Worthington isn't as awful as you think she is." Emma went to a different elementary school, so she never knew Reagan until we all started middle school together.

"Wait until you get to know her better. I've known her since kindergarten. Trust me. Reagan has a mean streak."

"Maybe she acts mean sometimes because she's insecure. Maybe that's why she's always bragging." Emma's dad is a social worker, so she's learning how to give people the benefit of the doubt. I've never been any good at giving people the benefit of the doubt. It's something I should probably work on.

"Insecure? Or maybe she truly thinks she's the most beautiful, the most popular, the most amazing girl in sixth grade, and that's why she's always bragging." Emma laughs, but I can tell she isn't convinced. I get the sense she's holding something back and all of a sudden, I think I know what it is. She's staring down at the carpet, and she stops petting Chester. "Wait. Are you two friends now or something?" I start braiding my hair, and my chest begins to hurt. I don't think it's the lasagna giving me heartburn.

"We're in the same group in my Chinese class, and she's nice. She invited me to go to this new restaurant with her family next Friday night." I hug my legs to my chest. Emma's too smart to fall for Reagan. That girl probably wants to be friends because Emma's mom is from China and Reagan thinks she can get help with her Chinese homework. Emma's too trusting.

I try to warn her. "Reagan Worthington can be nice one day, then turn on you the next day. One of the best things about middle school is not being stuck in the same class with Reagan all day long. I only have to deal with her once a day during math."

"Maybe you should give her a chance," Emma says. Thinking about Emma and Reagan hanging out, being friends, touches a nerve. The tears pour down my face out of nowhere. Like someone turned on an invisible tear faucet.

"Georgia, what's wrong?" Emma asks in a soft voice, which only makes me feel worse. Chester senses my sadness, too, and he trots over, snuggles into my lap, and tries to lick my salty cheeks.

"Is it because of Reagan?" I'm not crying about Reagan. And I don't want Emma to think I'm jealous or that she can't have other friends besides me. And so, I tell her. I tell her everything I know about my parents' fighting and my dad walking out the very day we brought Chester home.

"Georgia, my parents fight, too. That's normal. Your dad will be back, I'm sure of it." I like hearing those words, because they are exactly the words I need. "My dad works with married couples who fight all the time. He says it's worse when couples *don't* fight, because it means they're not dealing with their problems." That makes sense. Emma's smart, and her dad must know what he's talking about since helping people with their problems is his full-time job.

After Emma leaves, I join my mom and Chester who are cuddling on the living room couch. They're watching a documentary about Mr. Rogers. I snuggle up close to them. And then, like every other night since my dad left, I ask the same question. "Mom, when is Dad coming home?"

My mom's voice is gentle, and now she's petting my head instead of Chester's. "Don't worry, Georgia. We're working things out." But I have a hard time believing her. For one thing, my dad rented a small apartment about ten minutes away from our house. Even worse, I can hear Mom crying every night through my bedroom wall.

• • •

Early the next morning, I smell pancakes. I put on my robe and slippers and shuffle down the hallway. My mom's talking on the phone, and I freeze three feet from the kitchen. Even though she's trying to talk softly, I'm close enough to hear almost every word. No surprise, she's on the phone with her sister, my Aunt Felicia.

"Felicia, that man must hate me more than he loves his own daughter." The words pierce my heart like poison arrows. I tiptoe back to my room despite the lure of pancakes.

I know I was never meant to hear those words, but eavesdropping is the only way I'm able to get updates about my parents' marriage. My mom and dad are furious with each other. But I know my dad still loves us both. I believe he'll come back to us. I mean, so what if they argue? What does that prove? I get mad at my parents all the time, but of course I love them, and I'll always love them. That's how life works.

Chapter 8
Outlook Good

I'm having trouble sleeping. It's Sunday night, and my brain is a racecar, speeding around a track. I'm thinking about Emma and Reagan having a grand old time together, eating dinner with Reagan's parents at some fancy restaurant, practicing their Chinese at Emma's house with her mom's help. I'm tossing and turning in my bed, trying to get comfortable. Maybe I shouldn't have nagged my mom so much about getting a dog. Maybe I shouldn't have begged her to take me to the Humane Society. I love Chester with all my heart, but maybe getting a dog really *was* the last straw for my dad. Maybe it's all *my* fault he left.

I need to talk to someone, and Chester is a great listener. He never interrupts. And he gives you his full attention, like you're the most important person in the world. I turn on the lamp next to my bed. I tiptoe into the kitchen and quietly open Chester's crate. I carry his warm, sleepy body into my room and onto my bed. He's drowsy and sweet, and his paws smell like popcorn. He circles around a few times and settles down. I look into Chester's deep brown eyes and tell him about my mom's phone conversation with my aunt.

"What do you think, Chester? Will everything be okay with Mom and Dad?" Chester is looking right at me with those dark chocolate eyes, and I listen to him breathing for a long time as I pet him behind his ears and down his sides. He loves that. I don't expect an answer from Chester, but a sign would be nice. My body is relaxing, and I'm getting sleepy.

Suddenly, just as I'm about to fall asleep, Chester thinks it's playtime. Now he's the one who's wide awake. He jumps off the bed and runs over to the pile of dirty clothes in the corner of my room. I watch as he nudges around for a while, and then he finds my Magic 8 Ball underneath the mountain of laundry. Chester rolls that ball around with his wet nose. Then he sits back on his haunches with a satisfied look on his adorable face, and he barks twice. I'm worried my mom's going to wake up. She'll be angry I let Chester out of his crate.

I jump out of bed and creep over to him. "Shh! Chester, we don't want to wake up Mom!" I look down and read the words that appear in the window of my Magic 8 Ball. *Outlook good*, it says. Could this be the answer to the question I asked about my parents' marriage? I wanted to know if everything would be okay with Mom and Dad. *Outlook good.* Chester's wagging his tail. I wanted a sign, and he gave it to me. This is exactly the answer I'm looking for. I pull Chester onto my lap. I hold on tight to the message of hope floating in the inky blue liquid of my Magic 8 Ball. *Outlook good.* I can work with that.

Chapter 9
Probability

Dad takes me out to dinner every Wednesday. Chester and I stay at his apartment Saturday nights when Dad doesn't have a weekend shift at the hospital. I love being with him, but I don't like it when he calls Chester "Last Straw." It hurts that he thinks of Chester as the straw that broke the camel's back of my parents' marriage. Even though he refuses to call Chester by his real name, Dad can't hide the fact he's beginning to love that dog almost as much as I do.

Dad has a pull-out couch in his living room for Chester and me to sleep on. He's been living in this apartment for weeks, but there are still no pictures on the walls. The place has practically no furniture, and it doesn't look like he's in a hurry to turn it into a real home. Based on all the takeout containers in the refrigerator, I know he hasn't been cooking meals for himself.

I ask him the same question I ask every week: "When are you coming home?" And I get the same answer.

"It's not your problem, Georgia. Your mom and I are working things out. You worry about yourself and take care of Last Straw."

I've been working hard to fulfill all of my Humane Society promises. Chester has cooperated fully—not one poop accident in the house and only one minor pee accident at Dad's place. I cleaned it up so fast he never even knew it happened.

• • •

It's late Wednesday afternoon, my mom is grocery shopping, and my dad comes by to hang out with Chester and me before dinner. He's wearing a clean pair of emergency room scrubs because he has to go back to work later. It feels normal to see Dad sitting in his old chair. He's playing with Chester while I'm at the computer in the corner of the living room, working on a persuasive essay for my social studies class about lowering the voting age to thirteen.

Dad's here early because my parents are uncomfortable with the idea of letting me stay at home alone. Of course, I'm *not* alone, I'm with Chester, but still they think I'm going to set the house on fire or have a party or do something irresponsible. I guess they remember how wild they were when they were my age.

"Hey, Last Straw, how ya doing? You doing okay?" Chester's tail wags at fifty miles per hour while my dad rubs his belly. "How ya doing, big boy?" Dad's just being friendly. He certainly doesn't expect an answer. But there's something about Chester my father doesn't know. Chester loves to answer questions. All kinds of questions.

I've spent the last week asking that dog a ton of questions he answers with my Magic 8 Ball. I know it's hard to believe—and I don't expect to convince anyone, not even Emma, and especially not my dad—but Chester seems to have a special gift. It makes no sense, but I think my dog is a little bit psychic.

Maybe having a psychic dog is not as ridiculous as it sounds. Most dogs use their keen sense of smell to understand people's emotions. That's a scientifically proven fact. Chester has another *less common* canine ability. I think he can smell the future. Chester can predict what's going to happen, and he can communicate his predictions using my Magic 8 Ball.

"Hey, I'm running out to the car. Forgot something," my dad says. A minute later, he's back, and he's carrying a bag from Pets R Us. "Last Straw, look what I brought for you!" My dad pulls out a red rubber ball and bends down, holding it out for

Chester. Chester leaps onto his feet. He sniffs the new ball and sneezes. He shakes his head and then takes off down the hall in the direction of my bedroom.

"What's wrong with Last Straw?" my dad asks. "Doesn't he like his new ball?"

"Dad, stop calling him that. His name is Chester, and nothing's wrong with him. He's probably going to get one of his other toys." I'm trying to concentrate on my persuasive essay, but with my dad interrupting me every two minutes, it isn't easy.

Soon Chester's back in the living room, rolling the Magic 8 Ball with his front paws like he's a little soccer player. He's heading toward my dad, as though he's ready to make a goal. I give up on my essay so I can watch what happens next. The ball rolls to a stop at my dad's feet. Chester sits back on his haunches. Then he barks twice, as if to say, "Check it out!" I knew it. He's answering Dad's question.

My dad squats on the floor next to Chester and reads the answer on the Magic 8 Ball: "*Without a doubt.*" Chester starts wagging his tail again. Dad looks at me, his forehead scrunched. "So Last Straw would rather play with your Magic 8 Ball than this?" He picks up the red rubber ball and tosses it into the dining room. "Go on, go on, boy! Go get it!" Despite the excitement in my dad's voice, Chester ignores him, and he ignores the rubber ball bouncing in the other room. He looks at me, tilts his head, and furrows his brow as if he's thinking: *Why doesn't Dad understand?*

"Dad, Chester's trying to tell you something," I say.

"What's that supposed to mean? He's trying to tell me something with the Magic 8 Ball?" My dad's laughing. I need to move slowly, cautiously. I don't want to jinx Chester's prediction about my parents' marriage. When the time is right, I need to prove the same dog my dad calls Last Straw can predict the future for our family. But the time is not right. I decide to let Chester demonstrate his brilliance in another way.

"You asked Chester if he was doing okay, remember? That's when he ran to get the Magic 8 Ball. He told you he's okay. *Without a doubt*, that's what he's telling you."

My dad chuckles. "Or maybe he's telling me he doesn't like the smell of the new toy." Dad rolls the Magic 8 Ball in Chester's direction, but Chester's not interested in playing. "What's wrong, buddy?"

"Nothing's wrong with Chester. He's the smartest dog in the world. Watch this, Dad." I grab a penny from the bowl of loose change on the dining room table. I sit on the floor across from my dad with Chester between us.

"Chester, when I toss this coin, will it be heads? What's your prediction?" I put the Magic 8 Ball on the floor near Chester. He rolls it around the living room with his nose and then holds it between his paws with the small window facing up. "Read what it says, Dad."

My dad crawls over to Chester and leans down to read the message on the ball. "It says, '*Don't count on it.*'" I throw the penny up in the air, catch it, and slap it on the back of my hand, keeping the coin covered. Very slowly, I uncover the coin and show my dad the penny. "Tails," he says, laughing. "Nice trick, Last Straw."

"It's not a trick."

"Georgia, come on, you've studied probability in school." My dad gets up from the floor and walks away from us, into the kitchen. Chester and I follow.

"Yes, Dad, I know about probability, and it's not a trick, and it's not luck either. And his name is Chester not Last Straw."

"Please, Georgia." Dad's checking out the contents of the refrigerator, ignoring me. Then he holds up a bottle of cranberry juice, checking the sell-by date, because he doesn't trust my mom to get rid of old juices.

"Want some?" Dad asks.

"*Argh*. No, I don't want juice, and why won't you listen to me?" He pours himself a glass and walks back into the living room. Chester and I are at his heels.

I know what my dad means about probability. I've studied that subject every year since second grade. That's the problem with elementary school. They teach you the same thing year after year until you're ready for some serious math in middle school. But that doesn't stop my dad from lecturing me about the likelihood of the Magic 8 Ball's answers being accurate. He sits down on the couch.

"Georgia, please. Last Straw is a dog. He's a smart dog, no doubt about it. But, honey, he's still just a dog, right?"

Chester barks once and then rolls the Magic 8 Ball again, with his paw this time. I bend down to read the message that appears in the window. "*Yes, definitely*. Chester agrees with you. He knows he's a dog, Dad." Chester barks again. Maybe he's trying to tell *me* something, now.

"I'd better take Chester for a walk before we go out to dinner." I need to prove to my dad I'm responsible, that rescuing Chester should never have been the last straw that pushed him out the door—this dog is a wonderful addition to our family. My dad may not believe it yet, but Chester is more than smart. And even though I don't really believe in magic, there's something magical going on that I can't explain.

My dog can predict the future, and even Chester knows, it's time for my dad to come home again.

Chapter 10
What Happens At The Mall

Dad is super busy at work. He cancels Wednesday night dinner but then calls me the following Monday after school. He wants to go to the mall, which is weird. He hates that place almost as much as Mom does. I miss him, I don't have a ton of homework, and we both love the Mexican restaurant in the food court, so of course I say, "Why not?"

We're walking by a big department store on our way to the food court, when suddenly, my dad stops. He's staring at the mannequins in the window display, and he says, "Georgia, don't you need some new winter clothes?" *What is he talking about?*

"No. Besides, winter's almost over." My dad is in his own world. Little kids are lining up in the center of the mall so they can get their picture taken with the Easter Bunny, and he's talking about winter clothes.

We keep walking and pass a fancy shoe store. My dad stops again, like he's this big window shopper, which I know he's not. "How about some spring clothes or some new boots?" I figure he's feeling guilty for leaving us. My dad should know I'm not some clueless kid who doesn't even realize she's being manipulated. He *should* feel guilty. Buying me new boots won't fix anything. The only way to fix things is to move back home and to stop calling Chester "Last Straw."

"I have boots," I tell him. I grab his arm and try to pull him away. "Let's eat dinner. I'm starving."

"How about some designer boots. You know— UGGs or something?"

"UGGs? How do you know about UGGs?" My parents have zero interest in designer clothes, so I have no idea where this is coming from. That's when Dad's cell phone vibrates. He glances down to see who's calling. Maybe it's Mom, or maybe it's another emergency at work. He puts the phone back in his pocket without answering it. "Who was that?" I ask.

"Some robocall. Hey, I need to find the men's room. Be right back." I trail my dad as he sprints toward the restrooms, like he's not going to make it in time. But right before he turns the corner he slows down. He pulls out his cell phone, and it looks as though he's calling someone as he walks into the men's room.

I don't have to wait long. A few minutes later, my dad is smiling as he saunters in my direction, clearly feeling better. We head back out toward the food court, and already I can smell the enchiladas. My mouth is watering, but I'm curious. "Dad, how do you even know about UGGs?" I ask again.

"A friend of mine wears them."

"What friend?" I'm thinking I know all of my parents' friends, and I don't remember any of them wearing pricey designer boots. That's when my dad tells me about his "friend" Erin.

"Who's Erin?" I ask.

"She works with me at the hospital. An anesthesiologist in the ER."

I'm suspicious, and before I can force myself to count to ten, or even count to three, a dangerous question pops out of my mouth. "Is she your girlfriend?" My voice is quivering, but it must be loud because we've stopped walking and people are staring. I'm so terrified of my dad's answer that I'm not even embarrassed by the attention.

"Of course not. Erin's a friend. I've known her for over a year. You asked me how I knew about UGGs, so I told you." He starts to walk away, but I don't follow him. I stand my ground and talk loud enough for him and the world to hear me.

"Here's what I think: UGGs are too expensive and not worth the money. UGGs are ugly. That's probably why they're called UGGs—it's short for ugly. Can we please go home?" I spin around, heading back to the parking lot. My dad runs to catch up.

"What about dinner?" he asks.

"I'm not hungry. I want to go home."

I refuse to talk to my dad on the drive back. The car is cold, and I hold my arms crossed tightly in front of my chest, trying to warm up. I glare straight ahead. My dad's listening to some sports radio station which makes not talking much easier. When he pulls up in front of the house, he tries to explain. "Georgia, it's not what you think," he says. I don't even say goodbye, but I slam the car door extra hard.

Mom's in the living room with Chester, watching a cooking show on TV. I'm shaking with rage. I fall onto the couch, and my mom puts her arms around me. That's like unplugging the drain of the sink full of tears in my eyes. I tell her about Erin, dad's new "friend." I can't help myself. "She's a doctor at the hospital," I tell her. "An anesthesiologist!"

The celebrity-chef on TV is talking about how to debone a chicken with the right technique so none of the meat is wasted and how it all comes down to using the right knife. "Mom, can you please turn that off!" I can see right through the frozen smile on her face as she grabs the remote.

I try, but I can't stop sharing all the dreadful details. "I think she called him while we were at the mall, and he called her back, and he says they're just friends, but I don't know what to believe." I want my mom to tell me not to worry. She needs to say Erin's only a friend, and oh yes, she's Mom's friend too. But my mom puts her arms around me again and rocks me, like I'm a baby.

"And then I told Dad I wasn't hungry, and I made him take me home." I'm about running out of tears, and my stomach growls. "But the truth is, I'm actually starving, Mom." This part of the story makes her laugh.

"I'm glad you're hungry. Why don't you take Chester out for a walk? I'll start dinner," she says. "Now that I've learned how to debone a chicken." She's smiling, but I see right through her brave mask.

After the mall disaster with my dad, I keep pestering Chester about the future of my parents' marriage. I take out the Magic 8 Ball every morning, and every morning Chester reassures me. Will my dad move back home? *Outlook good.* Will my parents' marriage be okay? *Signs point to yes.* I want to believe in the magic. Like all kids, I suppose, I want to believe my parents will stay together forever. I want to believe in a happy ending. But it's not easy believing Chester when the future seems so *hazy*. And it's getting harder every day to believe my psychic dog's prediction of a happily ever after for this family.

forever. I want to believe in a happy ending. But it's
not easy believing Chester when the future seems
so hazy. And it's getting harder every day to believe
my psychic dog's prediction of a happily ever after
for this family.

Chapter 11
M&M's

Our math teacher, Mr. Burnett, introduces a new
unit, and it's all about probability and statistics. I'm
in no mood for this unit, especially since my
father's lecture about how probability explains
Chester's psychic abilities.

I tune out as soon as Mr. Burnett starts to talk.
I'm daydreaming about the time Mrs. Robins, our
fifth-grade teacher, gave each of us a small bag of
stale M&M's to teach us about probability. She
assumed we wouldn't be tempted to eat her leftover
Halloween candy from the last century. Of course,
everyone was tempted anyway, which was how we
discovered those chocolate candies were older than
the Grand Canyon.

Mrs. Robins' scratchy voice is impossible to
forget. "If I told you to reach into your bag of
M&M's—which you are *not* supposed to be eating,
Mr. Matthew Richardson. Don't make me tell you

again." Mrs. Robins raised her voice all the time, but never in front of other adults. She was one of those teachers who managed to control themselves when the principal walked in the room. "If I told you to reach into your bag and take one piece of candy, what is the probability you would choose a red M&M?"

My response to that question was *Who cares? Especially since the color has nothing to do with the taste. And especially since we're not supposed to eat them.* But like most of the kids in my class, except for Matt Richardson, I learned to squash those snarky responses like pesky mosquitos swarming around my ankles.

And then, as usual, a dozen fifth-grade hands would wave madly in the air. The probability of Mrs. Robins calling on one of *those* kids waving a hand in the air was zero. Not a chance. The probability of her calling on someone who didn't know the answer, or someone who was not paying attention, like me, was one hundred percent.

And here we are again. I thought math with Mr. Burnett would be an improvement. For one thing, he's a first-year teacher, and first-year teachers tend to be more enthusiastic. They think they can change the world. Also, Mr. Burnett looks cooler than most teachers I've known. He has a long beard but he's bald on top, which I guess is the look he's going for because he shaves his head. I hope Mr.

Burnett knows better than to dangle a bag of stale M&M's in our faces to prove a point about probability.

"Georgia." I look up. "Knock, knock! Who's there? Not Georgia," Mr. Burnett says. This is how he gets kids' attention when he knows they're daydreaming. "Will you please read the directions aloud?" He's wearing his eyeglasses on top of his shiny head, and I'm thinking they're going to slide right off. I can feel all eyes on me, and my face is warm. I sit up straight and figure out what he wants me to do. I look at the board and read.

"The Probability and Statistics Project: Think of an example from your everyday life when knowing about probability and statistics could be useful. Then write a word problem about it. Be prepared to present the problem to the class."

There are two reasons I like the assignment. One: It has nothing to do with stale M&M's. Two: Mr. Burnett practices what he preaches. He talks about math being useful and meaningful. Like me, he doesn't think filling out worksheets is meaningful.

"I'm going to give you a week to work on this for homework." Mr. Burnett knows what he's doing—he assigns homework he won't have to take home and correct every night. My mom, on the other hand, brings home a suitcase of assignments, quizzes, and tests she has to grade. Even good teachers like my mom can be their own worst enemy.

Mr. Burnett shares a rubric for our presentations. The first category is creativity, which matters a whole lot to Mr. Burnett. The other categories are accuracy and rigor.

The word rigor makes me think of dead bodies and rigor mortis. Who even uses the word rigor besides teachers? Undertakers maybe. Thinking about dead bodies makes me think about how competitive the kids in our math class can be with projects like this. Which brings me back to the topic of my least favorite person in sixth grade and everything Emma doesn't know about the real Reagan Worthington.

I need to quit daydreaming!

Chapter 12
The Sixth True Thing About Reagan Worthington

Here are five true things about Reagan Worthington:

1. Reagan Worthington thinks she's the most popular kid in sixth grade.
2. Last year she thought she was the most popular kid in fifth grade.
3. When she raises her hand in class, there's a fifty percent chance her answer has nothing to do with the teacher's question.
4. Her parents named all their kids after U.S. presidents.
5. Reagan's always surrounded by a million friends. (Obviously, when I use the word "million" I don't mean it literally. I'm talking about three or four or possibly five friends.) But my point is, she's never simply Reagan

Worthington walking or sitting or doing anything without her fans. That girl is never alone.

And now, Emma's part of the Reagan crowd. Ever since she went out to dinner with Reagan's family, that's all she talks about. Reagan this. Reagan that.

It's a rainy Saturday night, and we're at Emma's house in her family room, trying to find a movie we both want to watch that her mom will approve. "How about *Mean Girls*? Have you seen it?" I ask.

"Nope. What's it rated?" We're on opposite ends of her couch wrapped in comfy blankets, and the drumming of rain on the roof almost drowns out Emma's voice.

"Pretty sure it's PG-13."

"I don't know. It's an old movie, right? Is it black and white?" Emma asks.

"No, it's not that old. It's about a girl who reminds me of Reagan Worthington. I think you'd like it." Emma pulls herself up. She squints, looking at me with a mixture of sadness and worry.

"Georgia, you should give Reagan a chance," Emma says. "She's a lot of fun, and she likes you."

"What do you mean she likes me? She said that?" There's a clap of thunder, which makes us jump. I yank the blanket up under my chin.

"She knows you're my best friend, and she suggested we all hang out together."

"Ha! She acts as though she doesn't know me. Trust me, Emma. That girl has a mean streak."

Emma's mom comes in and asks if we want popcorn, and of course we want popcorn, so her mom says, "Coming right up."

While we wait for the popcorn, I decide to tell Emma the whole story. The sixth true thing about Reagan is this: I can't forgive her for what happened in fourth grade. I'm going to tell Emma all about it. She needs to know.

It was early in the year, probably September. Everyone had to write and share essays about how our parents chose our first names. Reagan said her parents named all the kids in her family after U.S. presidents. Her baby sister's name is Madison, and her brother's name is McKinley. Everyone calls him Mack. Reagan was named after Ronald Reagan. Her essay was a hard one to beat, and lucky me, I had to read mine next.

Why my Parents Named me Georgia

Lots of people think my parents named me Georgia because they wanted a son to name after my dad, whose name is George. The truth is they named me Georgia after the state. My dad hiked the entire

Appalachian Trail from Georgia to Maine before he married my mom. They met each other at the beginning of the trail in Georgia. It took him five months to hike all 2,200 miles. They got married in Maine five months later, at the end of the trail. I was born four months after that. And that's how I got my name.

Then, without even raising her hand, in front of everyone in the class, Reagan blurted out, "The state of Georgia? Were you conceived there?" Everyone in the class cracked up except our teacher, who said, "Reagan, that's none of your business." Everybody laughed even harder. I ran out of the room. I was so embarrassed I hid out in the girls' room until the bell rang.

That night, I asked my parents what Reagan meant by her question, and I got the *full* story. Turns out Reagan was right, but who cares? All I know is I'm lucky my parents didn't meet each other in Connecticut. That would be a mouthful for a first name.

I'm telling Emma the whole story, and she's hanging on every word. "Now you understand that forgiving Reagan for embarrassing me in front of the whole fourth-grade class would be impossible, right?"

Emma shrugs her shoulders, raises her eyebrows, and looks at me like she's waiting for more. "Really? That's it?" she asks.

"What do you mean?"

"Maybe she was curious and didn't mean to make fun of you. Or maybe you could forgive her." I can't believe what I'm hearing. I expected Emma to understand. I'm about to argue my point further, but her mom brings in a big bowl of popcorn, all buttery and salty and perfect. I realize I'm braiding and unbraiding my hair, which I'm going to have to quit doing if I want to eat.

"Thanks, Mrs. Miller," I say. I toss my braid over my shoulder and grab a handful of popcorn.

"Enjoy," she says as she's leaving the family room. I wait until I know she can't hear us talking.

"I can't believe you think what Reagan did was okay," I say.

"That's not what I think. I think… well, let me put it this way. My dad has a poster in his office with a picture of a flying eagle, and it says, 'Forgiveness… the ultimate freedom.'" Social workers like Emma's dad love animal posters that are supposed to be inspirational. "Don't you want to be free?" Emma asks.

"I'm pretty sure there are posters out there with pictures of scorpions that say 'Revenge… the ultimate satisfaction.' Let's face it, Emma, in life there are posters about everything. Hmm… *In life there are posters about everything.* Actually, that would make a great poster, too." Emma cracks up, which is one of the things I love about her. She thinks I'm funny, even when I'm not trying to be funny. Forgiving Emma is easy.

Chapter 13
Eavesdropping Again

Reagan's not the best math student in the world, but she pounces on this new assignment like a hungry bear on a birdfeeder. On Monday, I overhear her bragging in the sixth-grade hallway. I'm about four lockers away from her, trying to hide the fact I'm eavesdropping. She makes it easy for me, using her booming *I-don't-care-who's-listening* voice.

"I'm going to buy scratch lottery tickets for everyone in the class. Then I'm going to ask all the kids to figure out the probability of winning." I'm pretty sure she's too young to buy lottery tickets, but I keep my mouth shut.

"OMG, that's brilliant Reagan! You are so creative. Mr. Burnett is going to love that idea— you're going to get an A for sure," says Marisa, one of Reagan's minions.

Marisa's *"you're going to get an A"* prediction makes no sense. Mr. Burnett doesn't even give real grades. He uses the rubric so you know what you've done well and what needs improvement.

I'm pretending to search for something in my locker when I hear Emma's voice joining in with Reagan and Marisa. "Reagan, remember the story you told me, about your teacher who brought in the candy? That's what I'm going to do. I'm going to bring twenty old bags of stale M&M's from ten years ago, make everyone eat six handfuls and figure out the probability of kids barfing all over their desks." I can't believe what I'm hearing. *I* told Emma that story about Mrs. Robins. Why is she saying Reagan told her that story?

Marisa and Reagan burst out laughing when they hear Emma's idea. Even though I'm annoyed, I think she's funny too. I stop myself from laughing before they notice I've been listening in on their conversation.

After the sound of their giggles fades, I slam my locker shut and follow them to math class. I have my own ideas about this assignment. My vision for this math project is beginning to take shape in my mind. And it will definitely involve none other than the smartest dog in the world, and of course, a Magic 8 Ball.

I care about doing a good job with this assignment, but I have a more important goal. Once I can prove Chester is psychic, my dad will want to come home to our family. And now it's up to me to make that happen. With Chester's help, of course.

Chapter 14
Do The Math

Mr. Burnett's classroom is disorganized. This isn't a problem for me, but my mom would struggle with the mess. His desk is cluttered with school supplies and old papers, and he's the only teacher I know who doesn't believe in decorating bulletin boards. At the beginning of the year, he put up four math posters he bought at the Teacher Store, but even those posters are missing today.

He points to the empty wall in the back of the room. "As you can see, I've made space for you to display your math problems." Mr. Burnett's eyeglasses are sitting on his shiny head. "Let me explain how these presentations will work." He moves his glasses back in front of his eyes. "Each presenter will have five minutes to share the problem, and the class will have up to ten minutes to find a solution either independently or with a partner. Finally, the presenter will have five minutes to wrap it up. This gives each presenter up to twenty minutes." He must think kids can't add 5 + 10 + 5 on their own.

"I will evaluate each presenter based on the three categories from our rubric: creativity, accuracy, and rigor." Then, because he can't help himself, Mr. Burnett gives us another problem to solve.

"Class, how many days will we dedicate to the probability presentations? Do the math!" When Mr. Burnett says those three words, that's his signal for us to drop everything, turn, and work out the problem with our math partner. Fortunately, he reassigns new partnerships every month. This month my partner is Elliott Chestnut—the brainiac who lives two doors down the street from me. You have to love Elliott. He's definitely smart about lots of things, but he can be totally clueless about life.

It gets noisy in the classroom so fast, but not before Elliott whispers the answer to me. "Ten days. That's two school weeks." Then he turns back to his 750-page library book about the Revolutionary War. *Thanks, Elliott,* I think to myself, knowing I could have figured it out in about three seconds, but since Elliott figured it out in a fraction of one second, I lost interest in thinking for myself.

Mr. Burnett waits about a minute then calls on Emma, who gives him the correct answer. Emma's partner this month is Matthew, which won't help her math grade, but you can't be in a bad mood when you're working with Matthew. "That's correct, Emma. Ten days. We have twenty students in this class. Two students will present each day."

Mr. Burnett shuffles a deck of cards, and then he deals one card to every student in the room. He tells us to line up based upon the value of our cards. No talking allowed. "This is how we'll decide the order of the presentations," he says. "Ace is high, then king, queen, jack. Like bridge, my favorite card game, spades have the most value, then hearts, then diamonds, then clubs."

He writes all this on the board as he's talking so he doesn't have to repeat himself ten times. Mr. Burnett realizes lots of kids don't listen when teachers are giving directions. For a first-year teacher, Mr. Burnett knows what he's doing. He even knows better than to react when Matthew Richardson calls out, "What's bridge? Is that Go Fish for Old Geezers?" Mr. Burnett shakes his head and keeps on writing.

We're all shuffling around, showing each other our cards, pointing, and squeezing into the right places in the line. We're trying not to talk, but not talking doesn't mean we can't make other noises. There's a ton of giggling and grunting and finally I end up somewhere in the middle of the line with my card, the queen of diamonds. When Reagan picks the ace of spades, she screams like a vulture diving for dinner.

Wouldn't you know it, Matthew ends up with the joker. What are the chances? Mr. Burnett forgot to take the jokers out of the deck. He apologizes, but he's laughing along with everyone else. Then he gives Matthew another card. Unlucky Emma stands at the end of the line holding up her card. It's the two of clubs. By the time Emma gives her presentation, we will all be sick and tired of probability and statistics. I look back at her and shrug my shoulders, as if to say, "Oh well, someone has to go last." I'm happy that someone won't be me.

Chapter 15
Sunday Brunch

My parents used to invite company for Sunday brunch almost every other week. These days my mom doesn't entertain. And missing those Sunday brunches with friends and family is one more reason I want my dad to move back home where he belongs. I'm thrilled when my mom decides to have a Sunday brunch even without Dad. She invites Uncle Doug, Aunt Felicia, and my favorite cousin, Samantha.

I talk to Sam almost every day. Mostly we talk about my parents and Chester, but I haven't seen her whole family together since my dad moved out.

I give Chester a bath in the tub, using baby shampoo and being extra careful not to get any suds in his eyes. Chester keeps trying to escape the tub, putting his paws on my arms and trying to climb out. The tub's too slippery for him, and he keeps sinking back into the warm water. Finally, once he's all rinsed and squeaky clean, my mom picks him up and wraps him in some old towels, and we both rub him down. The second we let go, Chester shakes like crazy, giving me my own shower. Then he runs around the house. He rubs his ears on the living room carpet and rolls around on his back. Chester loves the hair dryer, though. He sits on my bedroom floor, closes his eyes, and doesn't move a muscle as my mom waves the warm air over his fur. By the time everyone arrives, he smells yummy and looks so handsome I have to take his picture.

"Chester!" Aunt Felicia goes crazy over all dogs, but she says Chester's her favorite.

"See, Mom, we should have gotten a dog years ago when I was Georgia's age. When I leave in August, you'll be so lonely!" My cousin is off to art school in the fall.

Sam has a tattoo on her shoulder, which is a copy of the artist Robert Indiana's LOVE sculpture. The letters L and O are on top of the V and E, and the letter O is tilted to the right. I think it's a cool tattoo, and the fact the artist's last name is a state—just like my name—makes it even cooler. Sam's parents were horrified and grounded her for a month because she got the tattoo without their permission. If I ever did that, my parents would ground me for ten years. Sam caught a break because she's an artist, and she got a full scholarship to an expensive college in Rhode Island.

Sam and I stuff ourselves silly with my mom's homemade waffles smothered with blueberries and real whipped cream. Chester sits near me under the table, even though everyone knows it's not okay to slip him anything to eat. He's not there to beg for food. He just likes to be where the action is.

No one is talking about my dad and how weird it is he's not sitting at the table. Everyone is trying to act all happy and light and breezy, but my mom is staring at her plate, and she barely eats half a waffle. My parents' relationship is the elephant in the room.

Later, Uncle Doug offers to do the dishes so Aunt Felicia and Mom can go off for a walk alone. They don't even take Chester with them. They probably want to talk about what's really going on with my parents' marriage.

Sam, Chester, and I hang out in my bedroom. Sam's on my unmade bed, trying to draw sketches of Chester, who is moving in circles on my blanket, trying to get comfortable. Poor guy is having trouble sitting still for his portrait.

"It's so weird without Uncle George here," Sam says. "I miss him." That's all it takes to release the flood of tears I've been holding back all morning. "Oh, Georgia, I'm sorry. I didn't mean to make you cry."

I sob into the sleeve of my sweatshirt. "I miss him so much. I want my family back!" Chester starts to whimper. He hates to see me unhappy.

"This is temporary," Sam says. "Your parents have had fights before. He'll be back, I know it." I wipe my face with the other sleeve of my sweatshirt.

I stretch out on the floor and put my hands behind my head. I'm staring at the cracks in the ceiling, trying to figure out how I can use Chester's psychic abilities and my math project to convince my dad to come home. I have the beginning of a plan floating around my brain, but there are missing pieces. Maybe Sam will have some ideas. I want to share my plan with my cousin, but there's no telling how she'll react. Finally, I decide it's worth the risk.

"Do you want to help me with my probability project?"

"Sure. Chester, please sit still," Sam moans. My cousin doesn't act interested in some dorky sixth-grade math project. I walk over and look at her sketch. It totally captures Chester's personality.

"Chester, go get the Magic 8 Ball," I say. Chester immediately jumps off the bed.

"Hey, Georgia, what are you doing? I need Chester to sit still so I can finish this sketch!"

"He needs a break, Sam, and besides, you said you'd help me with my probability project."

Chester finds the Magic 8 Ball under my desk. He rolls it over to me. He is such a good boy. I have to keep pinching myself to make sure I'm not dreaming—he's really *my* dog, part of *my* family.

"You won't believe what Chester can do. Watch this, Sam." I take a deep breath. "Chester, will my dad move back home? What's your prediction?" Chester rolls the ball around the room with his paws a few times until it comes to a stop with the window side facing up. I wait as the answer emerges from the hazy blue liquid. "Read what it says," I say. Sam puts her drawing down and walks over to where Chester and I are sitting.

"*Without a doubt*," Sam reads. "Nice, Georgia! See, Chester agrees with me. Uncle George will be back. Without a doubt!" I have my cousin's attention now.

"I know. But what are the chances? What's the probability of Chester giving me the right answer every time?"

"I'm not following you. Do you mean what are the odds the Magic 8 Ball will give you the answer you want to hear? That would depend."

"Depend on what?"

"First, you need to know how many positive answers and how many negative answers are inside," Sam says. She picks up the Magic 8 Ball and starts turning it around and reading the different answers. I already did some research, and so I give her the information she needs.

"There are twenty different answers. Ten are positive answers, like *You may rely on it* and phrases like that. And five are negative answers, like *Very doubtful*. And five are wishy-washy answers, like *Ask again later*," I tell her.

"If you always ask Chester questions needing a positive answer, you have a better chance of him getting it right," Sam explains.

"Duh! I know that. You have a one-in-two chance of getting a positive answer, and only a one-in-four chance of getting a negative answer."

"That's it?" Sam laughs. "That's your project?"

She's not impressed yet, but I'm about to wow my cousin. I'm about to rock her world to the core.

"Well, it's part of my project," I whisper. I'm trying to build the suspense. What I need is spooky music, like in the movies. "But here's the interesting part: Chester always gets it right, no matter what I ask him. And not only questions about my parents' marriage. He can predict the future!"

"Please, Georgia. That's impossible!" I want to tell my cousin I can trust Chester's predictions when the stakes are high, as with my parents' marriage. But first, I need to convince her that Chester can predict the future even when the stakes are low.

"Watch this." I grab a penny from my desk drawer where I keep my loose change, hair scrunchies, pencil stubs, leaky pens, broken sunglasses, and everything else in my life that fits in that junk drawer.

"Chester, I'm going to flip this coin," I say. "Will I get heads? What's your prediction?" Sam puts the Magic 8 Ball on the floor beside us, and Chester rolls it around in circles. When it stops rolling, he sits back on his haunches and barks two times.

"*My reply is no*," Sam reads.

"Okay. Here goes," I say. I flip the penny in the air and catch it in both hands. Then, with my right hand, I slap the coin onto the back of my left hand. I keep it covered for a moment, and slowly I move my right hand away to reveal the results of the coin toss. Sam looks down at the penny, then she looks at me. Then she looks at Chester, like she can't believe what she's seeing.

"It's tails," Sam says. Chester did it again, just as he did when I showed my dad. Exactly as he did when we practiced dozens of times before.

Sam tilts her head like she can't trust what she just saw with her own eyes. "Is that a trick? Let me try this time," she says. After six more trials with six different coins from Sam's own wallet, I'm pretty sure my cousin is convinced. I have an ally. Someone in my life is in on the secret.

"Sam, I've asked Chester about my parents. He's predicting the outcome is good for their marriage. I want to believe him. But I think I need to do my part, too. To help Mom and Dad get back together."

Sam is nodding her head, and suddenly it's as if a lightbulb went on in her brain. "I have an idea, Georgia," she says, her blue eyes twinkling.

"You do? Tell me!"

"Not yet. You need to trust me. I'll let you know as soon as I have all the details worked out. In the meantime, you work on your math project for school. Leave the rest to me." Tremors of excitement are churning in my stomach. It feels like an earthquake that barely measures on the Richter scale.

Sam grabs the sketch she made of Chester, and she's on her way out the door. "Georgia, I have a feeling your psychic dog is going to solve all of our problems!" All I can do, is hope she's right.

Chapter 16
From Rigor To Ridiculous

"Reagan, you're up first," says Mr. Burnett. I overheard Reagan talking to Emma on the way into class. She bought a new outfit and went to a hair salon last night so she'd look good for her presentation. Who does that? This is middle school, not kindergarten on Picture Day.

Flipping her shiny hair over her shoulder, Reagan bounces to the front of the room. She thinks she's a contestant on *America's Got Talent*. I rest my chin on the palms of my hands and settle in for the Reagan show.

"Okay, everyone. My presentation is about the odds of winning the top prize with a scratch-off lottery ticket. I was going to buy one for everyone in the class, even you, Mr. Burnett. But unfortunately, you have to be eighteen years old to buy lottery tickets."

"Ah, darn it! Not fair!" Matthew says.

"Don't worry, Matthew. I had my mom buy and scratch off all the tickets for us." Reagan holds up a large chart with two columns labeled NAMES and WINNINGS. The names of every kid in our class and our teacher are listed on the left-hand column of the chart. The information on the right-hand column is hidden with pink sticky notes.

"Okay, for this lottery game, there are six dollar-signs on each ticket you're supposed to scratch off. You need three of the same number to win. On the back of the ticket, it says your chances of winning are one in four, which sounds amazing, right? But it's not all that wonderful because the winning tickets could be for one dollar, five dollars, or ten dollars. There's only one prize for one thousand dollars. So, the problem for you to figure out is what are your chances of winning the thousand-dollar prize? Are there any questions?"

As usual, Matthew blurts out his question without raising his hand. "Do we get to keep the money?"

"Matthew, please raise your hand next time," Reagan says, like she's the teacher. "As I tried to explain, you have to be over eighteen to buy tickets or play the lottery. I wrote one name on the back of each ticket. My mom scratched off all the tickets to see who the winners would be. But this is just a presentation to learn something about probability in the real world. No one will be winning any money today." Some kids start booing, but Mr. Burnett shakes his head, and everyone quiets down.

Jordan raises his hand and waits. I guess he doesn't want to get in trouble with Reagan, who *actually believes she's the boss in charge of us.* "Yes, Jordan, thank you for raising your hand. Do you have a question?" This feels like preschool. I glance behind me at Emma, ready to roll my eyes at how ridiculous Reagan is acting, but I can't get her attention. She's taking this whole lottery ticket problem seriously. She's taking Reagan seriously.

"Okay, so if your mom scratched off the ticket with *my* name on the back, and that ticket won the thousand-dollar prize, does she have to share the money with me?" Jordan's question is pretty much the same as Matthew's, but I give Reagan credit for not sharing that fact with the universe.

"If my mom won the thousand dollars, she'd probably give this class a pizza party." Pizza? I glance at Emma again, with an *ARE-YOU-KIDDING?* expression on my face, but Emma's looking down at her notebook, scribbling something, and doesn't notice me trying to get her attention.

"Even if nobody in this class has a winning lottery ticket, as far as I'm concerned, you are all winners!" Reagan says. "That's why I've brought prizes for everyone." She holds up a grocery bag. "Any other questions? Last chance, everyone."

Reagan probably practices being an annoying, bossy teacher with her stuffed animals. She probably lines up her little stuffed bears and tigers and puppies in straight rows at the foot of her bed. I'd bet all of my future lottery winnings she lectures them about appropriate behavior before she goes to sleep each night.

Mr. Burnett has a question. "Reagan, do you know how many tickets the lottery made for this particular game?"

"Yes, Mr. Burnett, they made four million tickets for this game."

Elliott raises his hand. Reagan looks at the clock and sighs with more drama than an actor in a bad movie. "Yes, Elliott—and this is the last question, everyone."

"One in four million."

"Excuse me?" Reagan is annoyed.

"That's the answer. You have one chance in four million. One chance of winning the thousand-dollar prize. You already told us—they made four million tickets, and there's only one prize worth a thousand dollars."

You don't have to be a brainiac like Elliott to figure that out. And I don't need a Magic 8 Ball to predict Reagan scored a Needs Improvement in the rigor category for her probability project.

Matthew shouts out again, "Are you kidding me? One in four million? What a waste of money.

Reagan, you and your mom threw away twenty dollars!"

Everyone is talking and laughing while Reagan's face turns from rosy red to blotchy purple. I think she's about to cry. There's nothing worse than crying in class. Everyone will talk about you for weeks, although barfing is pretty bad, too. I guess if I had to choose between crying and barfing—I'd choose crying. I hope Reagan doesn't cry and barf at the same time. I feel sorry for her, but I'm also thinking, *Now she knows how it feels.*

Mr. Burnett walks to the front of the class. "Okay, okay, settle down, people. Here's an important question: If the odds of winning a big prize are so terrible, why do you think people keep buying lottery tickets?" The class is silent. Even Matthew is speechless.

"Reagan, I want to thank you for giving us something important to think about," he says. "If people understood probability, would they buy lottery tickets with their hard-earned money? Take out your math journals, everyone. Spend the next ten minutes writing about these very thought-provoking issues. And then Reagan will share the prizes she brought as well as the results of her lottery ticket experiment."

As we're writing, Reagan's face returns to normal, if you call a smug, self-righteous, and full-of-herself face normal. Everyone's in a forgiving mood as she hands out bags of Skittles and erasers in the shape of dollar bills. And surprise, surprise, when she removes the sticky notes from the right-hand column of the chart, we learn no one in our class has the thousand-dollar ticket. Marisa's ticket won a dollar, which given the odds, is plain bad luck. And a dollar isn't nearly enough for a slice of pizza let alone a pizza party.

Chapter 17
Doug's Mugs

Early Saturday morning, my cousin drives me to Uncle Doug's coffee shop in the center of town. Sam tells me she has a surprise. The only clue she gives is that her surprise has something to do with using Chester's gifts in a way that will solve both of our families' problems.

I understand what she means. Her family's problems have nothing to do with marriage and everything to do with money. My uncle named his coffee shop Doug's Mugs for a good reason: he makes all of the mugs on his pottery wheel in his garage, and he glazes them with different colors and textures. Even though Uncle Doug is a gifted potter, and he uses his own special blend of coffee beans, his business has been slow lately. There are already a zillion coffee shops in the world, and every time you turn around, another one pops up on a different street corner. The competition is fierce.

We walk into the shop and march up to the counter where Uncle Doug is organizing his display of mugs. "What will it be today, lovely ladies?" he asks. We're the only customers in the shop, except for an older couple reading newspapers on the old leather couches near the window.

"Hot chocolate for me," I say. "With whipped cream, please."

"The usual for me, too, Dad." Sam's usual is a large double cappuccino made with skim milk.

Sam and I settle at a back table to wait. "So, tell me! What's the surprise?" I ask.

"Wait for Dad," she says.

"Tell me now," I beg. But Sam won't budge. She ignores me, texting someone on her cell phone while I braid and unbraid my hair ten times. Finally, Uncle Doug carries over two steaming mugs and pulls up a chair. Sam puts her phone away. I can tell Uncle Doug has something important on his mind. He doesn't waste time with his usual small talk.

"Sam told me about that coin-toss trick you did with Chester," Uncle Doug says. "Although I'm not convinced Chester's special gift is anything other than luck, Sam had an idea. She suggested we include Chester and your Magic 8 Ball in our new advertising campaign. What do you say?"

I have no idea what Chester and my Magic 8 Ball have to do with advertising for Doug's Mugs Coffee

Shop. This must be Sam's so-called surprise, but it makes no sense. How will this help my parents' marriage? "I'm lost. What are you talking about, Uncle Doug?" I ask.

"Sam, show Georgia your sketch," he says. She pulls out a sketchpad from her backpack. Sam shows me a sweet drawing of Chester, one paw resting on the top of a huge Magic 8 Ball, almost as big as Chester, a steaming mug of coffee next to him. Under the picture is the caption:

Doug's Mugs: Best coffee in the world?
Without a doubt! You may rely on it! It is certain!

Uncle Doug and Sam are perched on the edge of their chairs, waiting for my reaction. "Chester could even do a TV commercial," Uncle Doug says. "I'd say, 'Welcome to Doug's Mugs. Do we have the best coffee in the world? What do *you* think, Chester?'" Uncle Doug uses a sappy, deep, dramatic commercial voice. "Then Chester would roll the Magic 8 Ball around with his paw, and the camera could zoom in on the Magic 8 Ball. The message would read: *Signs point to yes!*"

Sam jumps in. "And then Chester would bark, like he did in your room, and then the camera could zoom in to get a close-up shot of a hot mug of steaming coffee. What do you think, Georgia?" I don't know what to think. They're both so excited. I want to help Uncle Doug with his coffee shop business, and I don't want to burst their happy bubble. I need more information. But all I can think to say is the absolute worst thing in the world.

"Well, what if Chester doesn't think Doug's Mugs Coffee Shop has the best coffee in the world?" My uncle and cousin are speechless. I try to undo the damage. "What I mean is, what if he rolls the Magic 8 Ball and the response is *Very doubtful* or *My reply is no*?"

"We would try again until we got a positive answer, right?" Uncle Doug says, looking at me as though I sprouted a second head. Uncle Doug doesn't believe Chester is psychic. He doesn't believe Chester is truly predicting the future, using the answers on my Magic 8 Ball. To Uncle Doug, it's only about getting more customers for his coffee shop.

"Well, what about *truth in advertising*?" I say. "Isn't there a law about that?"

"I think Doug's Mugs has the best coffee in the world, don't you?" Sam asks. Now I'm really feeling guilty. I insulted my cousin and my uncle, and all they want from me is permission to use Chester for a TV commercial.

"Look, I don't drink coffee, but I'm sure your coffee is great, Uncle Doug. Your hot chocolate is amazing. But Chester doesn't drink coffee or hot chocolate. How can he know for sure?"

Uncle Doug shrugs his shoulders. "Tell you what, Georgia, think about it for a day or two. I believe Chester could help our business. You know how slow it's been lately. And who knows, we could make Chester rich and famous. Anything is possible, right?"

Uncle Doug goes back to work, leaving Sam and me alone at our table. I shrug my shoulders. "I want to help, Sam. I just don't see how this plan solves my family's or your family's problems."

"My dad's talking about having to close the coffee shop. Business is slower than usual. Look around." She waves her hand around the quiet shop. "The timing couldn't be worse with me going off to art school next year. Even with my scholarship, there's living expenses, books, and supplies. My parents aren't sure we can afford it."

I can't believe Sam may have to give up her art school dream. That's all she's been talking about for four years. When she got accepted to her first-choice school, we had a huge family celebration.

"And you think Chester can make a difference?" I ask.

"I know Chester can make a difference!" She must sense I'm on the edge of the diving board, ready to jump into the pool, ready to agree to anything. All I need is a gentle push.

"And, Georgia, this could be the beginning of Chester's career in advertising. If your dog becomes rich and famous, Uncle George will realize Chester wasn't the 'last straw' but the best thing that ever happened to your family." I think about the odds of this plan working and realize there's absolutely no way I can predict the outcome. But if we can convince my dad Chester really is the best thing that ever happened to our family, if there's even a small chance, it's worth a try.

"Okay," I say, nodding my head. "We'll do it. *Signs point to yes!*"

Chapter 18
What Are The Odds?

"Okay, everyone. What are your odds of getting a divorce?" Beth Lagrasse asks. Whoa. I didn't see that one coming. I watch as Beth moves to the side of her poster, revealing a picture of a fancy wedding cake decorated with colorful question marks and the words *Till Death Do Us Part?* Underneath the wedding cake she wrote two words: *It depends!* She certainly has my attention.

After days of gambling and sports-related probability presentations, the topic of divorce is a change of direction, but not a welcome change. The last topic I want to think about is divorce. I'm wondering if Beth's family is going through the same thing we're going through.

"Zero chance I'm ever getting divorced," Matthew calls out, "because there's zero chance I'm ever getting married!" The class erupts in laughter. Mr. Burnett jumps in, taking the topic of divorce seriously. He walks over to where Beth is standing in front of her poster, and he holds up his hand. That's all it takes with Mr. Burnett. Everyone quiets down.

"Beth, give us more information. I'm assuming you're asking about the odds of getting a divorce for people who are already married or planning on getting married. Am I correct?"

"Yes, Mr. Burnett, that's right. What are the odds of getting a divorce for people who get married before the age of twenty-two compared with people who get married after the age of twenty-two?" Then Beth takes a black marker and writes the number one, and next to that she writes the word AGE in big capital letters.

Twenty-two. Is that a magical marriage number? My dad was twenty-four when he met his future wife, Carrie Ann Cohan. Carrie Ann was only nineteen years old. Their wedding was right before my mom's twentieth birthday. What if one person is under twenty-two and one is over twenty-two? That's what I want to know. I'm not about to raise my hand and open up that can of worms.

Besides, I don't want to think about the probability of my parents splitting up for good. I have to believe that with Chester's help, they'll find their way back to each other, to the life we had before my dad left home. Before the last straw broke the camel's back of my parents' marriage.

"Beth, is this a math problem, or are you simply asking the class to take a wild guess?" Mr. Burnett asks.

"My parents are divorce attorneys, and they're always working. They work late most nights, and usually one or both of them go to the office on weekends because they have so many clients." So, that's why Beth chose this problem. At least her parents aren't getting a divorce. I lean in, ready to listen closely. I might as well learn as much as I can.

"Give us more information, Beth," Mr. Burnett says.

"It seems so many couples are getting divorced these days. I studied this problem for my project, and I can tell you the odds are worse for people who get married when they're young," Beth says.

I don't like what I'm hearing. I want to cover my ears with my hands, squeeze my eyes shut, and scream, "I can't hear you! I can't hear you!" like I used to do when I was a toddler being told to take a nap.

Elliott raises his hand. "Elliot?" Beth calls on him right away rather than answer Mr. Burnett's question about whether we were supposed to do the math or take a wild guess. I'm thinking there is no way we can figure out this problem without a large sample of marriage and divorce data including the ages of the brides and grooms when they tied the knot. Beth didn't prepare for this very well.

"Fifty percent of all marriages end in divorce," Elliott says.

"Thank you, Elliott, but fortunately for married people, you are WRONG!" It's nice to know Elliott can be wrong sometimes. It happens so rarely. "People *think* the odds of getting divorced is one in two, but that's false," said Beth. "It's actually 43 percent for all marriages. But the odds are worse for people who get married before age twenty-two— it's 46.6 percent for those couples. And it's even worse for people who don't get a college education—it's like 68.8 percent for those couples." Beth writes the number two on her poster, and next to that she writes EDUCATION. "Any questions?"

This is a lot to think about. And YES, I have a question. Fortunately, both of my parents went to college. My mom tied the knot with my dad before she finished her degree, but when I was a baby, she went back to school part time. She even earned her Master's degree in teaching before I started kindergarten. What does it mean for my parents' chances of staying married? I can't possibly ask that question in front of all the kids in my class.

I can feel my teacher's shadow as he hovers near my desk. He can sniff out kids who daydream like a polar bear sniffing out his dinner through three feet of ice. "You've found some interesting statistics, Beth. Not that we need another reason to get a college education folks, but there you go," says Mr. Burnett. "Thank you, Beth, for sharing another way math can help us make important decisions in our lives."

Even though there's no actual math problem to solve, Mr. Burnett makes us write for ten minutes about why learning math will make our lives better.

• • •

Later that day, Emma and I are eating lunch in the cafeteria, sitting with a bunch of kids from her Chinese class, including Reagan Worthington. They're practicing vocabulary, which of course, leaves me out of the conversation. It doesn't much matter, because I'm sitting there lost with my turkey sandwich, thinking about Beth's presentation.

I can't get those numbers out of my head. 43 percent, 46.6 percent, 68.8 percent. I can't stop thinking about how furious my parents are with each other, and how my dad's living in his own apartment, and how maybe he's dating some anesthesiologist who wears UGGs. Ugh! Maybe Chester and the Magic 8 Ball were wrong. Maybe the outlook for my parents' marriage isn't good enough. And maybe the odds of me getting out of this miserable mood before I finish my turkey sandwich, which is sticking to the roof of my mouth, is close to zero percent. I get up to throw the rest of my lunch away, and no one at the table says a word, not in Chinese and not in English, either.

Chapter 19
Possible

After Beth's presentation on the odds of divorce, I'm in a rotten mood. All I want to do is take Chester for a long walk and then curl up on my bed with a book.

I'm *not* looking forward to my mom's usual "How was school today?" greeting, the second I walk through the door. You'd think she'd shake things up once in a while. Maybe she could try asking me something more interesting. She's the most predictable parent in the universe.

As I let myself in the back door, I *am* looking forward to seeing Chester. He greets me every day by barking wildly as though we've been separated for ten months. That dog practically does backflips to let me know how much he's missed me. But I don't hear a sound. No barking and no "How was school today?" My mom isn't in the kitchen talking to Aunt Felicia on the phone. She isn't in the pantry alphabetizing the spices. She isn't in the living room reshelving the books according to the color on their spines. She isn't in the bathroom labeling categories of items in the medicine cabinet.

It isn't like my mom to take naps in the afternoon after work, but my parents' bedroom door is closed. I walk down the hallway and knock. "Mom—you in there?" I hear some muffled sobbing noises. It doesn't take a fortune-telling dog with a Magic 8 Ball to know why she's crying. The sound breaks my heart, but I knock again, "Mom?"

"You can come in, Georgia." I open my parents' bedroom door. I still call it that—my parents' bedroom—even though my dad hasn't been living here for a while. The room is dark, and I can barely see anything until my eyes adjust. The window blinds are closed, and my mom is curled up on the bed with Chester at her side. Mom's eyes are swollen. Her face looks puffy, as though she's been suffering from pollen allergies. I sit down on my dad's side of the bed, and Chester moves over to me. He licks my face, wags his tail, and then rolls over on his back so I can rub his soft belly.

"Mom, are you okay?" I know I asked the silliest question I could ever ask someone who is clearly an emotional wreck.

"Oh, Georgia, I'm sorry. I don't want you to see me like this."

"It's okay, Mom. Did something happen?" Another silly question.

"I miss him so much," she says. "I don't know what to do." She starts sobbing again, her face pressed into the pillow to mute the sound. "I think he wants a divorce, and I'm pretty sure he's seeing someone else!" Mom keeps on crying, breaking my heart into smaller and smaller pieces.

I have no idea what to say. I'm just a kid. All I know is that the odds of my parents' marriage ending in divorce is 46.6 percent because Mom was too young when they got married. But my mom doesn't need to know that statistic. I want her to stop crying. I want her to feel better. I want to increase the odds of a happy ending for this family. And so, I say something truly desperate.

"Do you want me to talk to Dad? Maybe I can convince him to come home. I mean, it's my fault he left. If I hadn't forced you to go to the Humane Society, maybe he'd still be here. Poor Chester was the last straw, and it's all my fault." My mom stops sobbing; she wipes her face and her drippy nose with the back of her arm. I'm too miserable to be grossed out, but I hand her the box of tissues from the nightstand. My mom pulls herself up and leans her back against the headboard. She gazes at me and shakes her head.

"Oh, Georgia. That's not true. Dad's leaving had nothing to do with you. He's teasing when he calls Chester 'Last Straw.' He didn't leave because we adopted a dog," she says, tears staining her cheeks.

And then I'm crying, too, because the burden on my shoulders is so heavy it hurts. My mom puts her arms around me and gives me this long hug, rubbing my back, and saying, "It's going to be okay, Georgia. It's going to be fine."

I look over at Chester who's drifted off to sleep, blissfully unaware of all this drama. I don't know how he does it. I love that dog so much; just watching him and listening to him breathe makes me feel better. My mom's hug helps, too.

I know it's too soon to tell her, but I remind myself even though Dad left when we brought Chester home, maybe my amazing psychic rescue dog will help me bring Dad back again. Maybe that's not probable, but it is possible.

Chapter 20
Chester Goes to School

Fortunately, my principal gives us permission to bring Chester to school. No one in my class is allergic, and the fact that my dog has no teeth works in our favor. Dad has a later shift at the hospital, and he agrees to bring Chester to the classroom. My plan is falling into place. After Dad sees my probability project, I'll be ready to tell him about Chester's prediction for our family. Then he'll be more likely to believe it.

Elliott gives his presentation before mine. I'm so nervous I can't stop braiding my hair as Elliott tells us about eye color, genetics, and the odds of having blue eyes. Even though everyone in my family has brown eyes, I have to admit his presentation is interesting, and as far as rigor is concerned, it's off the charts.

Elliott's going to be a hard act to follow. Mr. Burnett's beaming. He's probably thinking about the day when his star student wins a Nobel Prize in twenty years. He'll be bragging to all his friends, "I had that kid in my sixth-grade math class!"

I look up and see my dad's face in the window of our classroom door. He's waiting for a sign from me.

"Georgia, are you and Chester ready?" Mr. Burnett asks. I signal to my dad it's time. All eyes are on my amazing dog as he walks through the door. Chester's carrying my old stuffed animal in his mouth, and I notice that Dottie the polka-dotted dog needs a bath. Lots of kids are putting their hands out as Chester walks by, trying to pet him, but he marches right up to Reagan's desk and drops Dottie in her lap. Then he starts sniffing inside Reagan's desk and pulls out a half-eaten chocolate bar.

"Argh! Disgusting!" Reagan shrieks and jumps up. Drool-covered Dottie falls from her lap to the floor. I pull the chocolate bar out of Chester's mouth and give it back to Reagan. Most kids are laughing, but I know chocolate is unhealthy for dogs. I grab Dottie and hand her over to my dad. Then he gives me Chester's blanket and a bag of dog-treats for later.

"Good luck," Dad whispers. I think he's talking to me, but then I notice he's looking right at Chester. *Gee, thanks, Dad.* I watch as he strolls to the back table and pulls up a chair.

"Why's his tongue hanging out of his mouth like that?" Matthew calls out.

"Chester doesn't have any teeth," I say. As if on cue, Chester pulls his tongue back in his mouth. You've got to love that dog.

"No teeth? Grandpa has no teeth? What an old geezer!" Matthew says, making everyone laugh. Reagan's laughing the loudest.

"Settle down," Mr. Burnett says.

"Well, I think he's cute," Emma says as I pull out my Magic 8 Ball.

"Does everyone know what this is?" I ask. A bunch of hands wave in the air. "Emma." I call on her because A) she's still my best friend even though she's fallen under Reagan's spell, B) she stuck up for Chester, and C) I know she won't give a sarcastic answer.

"It's a Magic 8 Ball. You ask it a question and turn it around and it will give you an answer," Emma explains. Emma knows I used to ask my Magic 8 Ball if I'd ever get a dog. But she doesn't know about Chester's psychic skills. Not yet.

"That's right, but you have to ask a yes-no question. If I flipped a coin like this"—I flip a penny in the air, catch it, then slap it on the back of my left hand, keeping the coin covered— "and then if I ask the Magic 8 Ball 'Is it heads or tails?' that wouldn't work. It's not a yes-no question. But if I ask 'Is it tails?' what's the likelihood of the Magic 8 Ball being correct?" Four kids raise their hands. I call on Elliott because I want a reasonable answer.

"If you ask a person, you'd have a fifty-fifty chance of it being heads or tails each time. You divide the number of desired outcomes by the total number of possible outcomes," Elliott says. I think he's already lost most of the kids in my class, and I can hear Matthew fake-snoring in the back of the room. "But asking the Magic 8 Ball instead of a person is more complicated. We need more information." Mr. Burnett's eyes practically pop out of his head. That man lives for what he calls "teachable moments."

"Elliott is correct. Turn to your math partner and talk about this. What information do we need in order to calculate the likelihood of the Magic 8 Ball accurately answering the question: 'Is it tails?'"

I notice my dad checking his phone, and I worry he's not paying attention. Meanwhile, Chester must be getting bored. He's dozing on his blanket. His eyes are half closed, and his tongue is slipping out of his mouth again. The buzz in the room lulls Chester to sleep. His leg starts to twitch; he growls and snaps at some invisible rabbit he's probably chasing in his dream.

After a few minutes, Mr. Burnett gets all the kids' attention with his booming voice and wakes up Chester, too. My dad even puts his phone away.

"Georgia, students want to know how many of the answers in the Magic 8 Ball are 'yes,' or affirmative, and how many are 'no,' or negative. Do you have the information we need?"

I tack my poster to the bulletin board and read my Magic 8 Ball problem and the possible answers.

The Magic 8 Ball Problem

Problem: If Chester rolls the Magic 8 Ball, what's the probability of him correctly predicting whether Mr. Burnett gets heads or tails on ten coin-tosses in a row?

20 Possible Answers:

10 possible answers are positive *(Yes definitely, Outlook good, etc.)*

5 possible answers are negative *(Not a chance, Outlook not so good, etc.)*

5 possible answers are neither *(Ask again later, Cannot predict now, etc.)*

"Whoa! Ten coin-tosses in a row?" Mr. Burnett's eyes bulge, and his eyebrows disappear into the crease on the top of his forehead. "This problem just got much more complicated!"

Reagan raises her hand but doesn't wait for Mr. Burnett or me to call on her. "There's a fifty-fifty chance you'll get heads or tails," she blurts out.

"And dogs can't make predictions, so it's a stupid problem." You do not use the word "stupid" in Mr. Burnett's classroom. My teacher pounces.

"This happens to be a very difficult problem to solve. Besides, there are no stupid problems and no stupid questions. Reagan, please see me after class." Mr. Burnett's comments make me so happy I could hug him for defending me.

"Mr. Burnett," I say. "The probability of getting either heads or tails with any coin toss is fifty-fifty, or one in two, just as Elliott and Reagan said. It doesn't matter how many times you toss the coin. But with all the different possible answers in a Magic 8 Ball, getting it right even once is less likely."

"Can you give us an example, Georgia?"

"Let's say you ask Chester if he predicts the answer will be tails, but you toss the coin and get heads. There's only a one-in-four chance the Magic 8 Ball will give Chester the answer he needs. In this case he needs one of the five negative answers because it's not tails. And predicting correctly ten times in a row would be even more difficult."

"Excellent point, Georgia. I'd venture to say getting it right ten times in a row with a Magic 8 Ball is so unlikely that it's virtually impossible," Mr. Burnett says.

"Hmm. Impossible? I wouldn't say impossible, Mr. Burnett." I can't believe how confident I sound. My stomach is churning, and my palms are so sweaty I'm terrified the Magic 8 Ball is about to slip out of my hands and crash on the floor. "I agree it's unlikely, but I *know* it's possible," I say.

"Predicting the correct answer with a Magic 8 Ball ten times in a row?" Mr. Burnett says. "Chester would have to be psychic."

"It's unlikely, it's improbable, it's doubtful… but it's *possible* for Chester to accurately predict heads or tails ten times in a row with my Magic 8 Ball. It must be possible, Mr. Burnett, because, you see… Chester can do it," I say. "And this amazing dog is about to prove just that!"

Chapter 21
Without A Doubt

At first, the room is silent. Then Matthew yells out, "A psychic dog? This I gotta see!" Everyone starts talking at the same time.

"Okay, people," Mr. Burnett says. "Settle down. We don't want to run out of time. Chester's been waiting patiently, so I'm going to let you continue your work on this challenging math problem for homework tonight."

Reagan complains in a loud whisper, "Perfect! Just what we need. More homework! Thanks, Georgia!"

"Now, let's have some fun! Chester, time to help us out," our teacher says. Chester opens one eye and slips his tongue back into his mouth. I clap my hands a few times to get him in a playful mood. It's time to wow the class and Dad with my dog's probability prowess.

"Let's go, Chester," I say. The kids gather on the rug in the corner of the room. Mr. Burnett takes a coin out of his pocket. My dad is leaning up against the wall, but he's paying attention.

"Chester, when I flip this coin, will I get tails?" Mr. Burnett asks. I place the Magic 8 Ball with the window facing down in front of Chester. We wait. It's so quiet in the classroom I can hear my heart pounding. My mouth's so dry my tongue sticks to the roof of my mouth. Everyone's looking at Chester, who's gazing up at me, not knowing what to do. "Go ahead, Chester. What's your prediction? Will it be tails?" Mr. Burnett asks again. Some kids giggle. Reagan's whispering to Matthew, but I can't hear what she's saying.

"Chester," I say. "Are you ready?" He looks at me, turns his head around to look at my dad, then Mr. Burnett, then gazes back at me. So much depends on Chester cooperating.

"Come on, Chester," I plead. I'm holding my breath. "You can do it." Finally, he noses the Magic 8 Ball back and forth a few times and then stops it with his paw, making sure the window is facing up. He sits back on his haunches. All the kids near the ball lean over to see what it says.

"*It is certain,*" two kids read the message at the same time.

"So, Chester is certain it's going to be tails. Let's see if he's right." Mr. Burnett flips his coin in the air, catches it with his right hand, and slaps it down on the back of his left hand. As he lifts the hand that's hiding the coin from view, he bends down to show Matthew.

"It's tails!" Matthew shouts. "Grandpa did it! The old geezer did it!" he shouts even louder. Everyone starts high-fiving each other. "Go, Grandpa! Go Grandpa!" a few kids are chanting.

"His name's not Grandpa, it's Chester," I say.

"Well, he doesn't have teeth, so he's Grandpa to me," Matthew says, making everyone in the class crack up. Even my dad's chuckling.

"Let's try it again," Emma says. Kids clap and cheer, but as soon as Mr. Burnett starts to talk, the room is silent again.

"Chester, when I flip the coin again will it be heads this time? What's your prediction?" Chester doesn't make us wait. He rolls the ball around in a small circle a few times before making it stop again with the window facing up. He barks twice. Slowly the message appears in the small window.

Elliot sees it first. "*My reply is no!*" he says. We all watch Mr. Burnett as he flips the coin again. He removes the hand that's covering the coin and bends down to show Beth.

"It's tails," she says. Everyone cheers. "That's two times in a row!" Emma yells. By the fourth successful trial, Matthew insists we use a different coin. Then on the sixth trial, Elliot wants to flip the coin himself because kids think Mr. Burnett is in on the trick.

The odds may be against Chester predicting every answer correctly ten times in a row. But despite the odds, he does it. And after ten different trials, using four different coins and four different coin flippers, the class is going wild. Kids are pumping their fists in the air, and everyone's cheering together. *Grandpa! Grandpa! Grandpa!*

By the time the bell rings, both my dad and Mr. Burnett are scratching their heads. They keep looking at each other as if to say, "Could this really be happening?" Mr. Burnett watches me closely as I give Chester some bacon-flavored treats. I hug that dog like there's no tomorrow, burrowing my face in his fur. "Good boy, Chester," I say. "You are the best dog in the world. Definitely, the best dog. *Without a doubt.*"

As my dad collects Chester, the blanket, and the leftover treats, he leans in and whispers, "I don't know how you did that, Georgia. That's one heck of a trick."

"It's not a trick. Chester's psychic. He can tell the future with my Magic 8 Ball," I say, all smiles.

"Right," Dad laughs. "A psychic dog. If you say so." I fly out the door. I'm late for my next class, but nothing can ruin my mood.

Chapter 22
Dinner With Dad

It's finally warm enough that I don't need my winter jacket. Tulips and daffodils sprout from our garden. A yellow coat of pollen blankets our car. Chester welcomes the longer days for hanging out at the dog park and playing frisbee in the backyard.

On Wednesday night, my dad takes me to Roberto's for pizza. This is the first time in a while I get to be alone with him for long enough to have a real conversation. Now that Dad has seen proof of Chester's psychic abilities, it's time for Part II of my plan.

Emma helped me figure out the right questions to ask, worded exactly the right way. I wrote them on an index card and stuffed them in the back pocket of my jeans. *When are you coming home, Dad?* That will be my first question. I wanted to ask *Are you and Mom getting a divorce?* but Emma said to stay away from that question. She said I need to stick with the questions that assume he's coming home.

After the waiter takes our order, Dad brings up the topic first and gives me the opening I need. "Georgia, I want to talk to you about Mom and me, and why I left when I did." I practically choke on my breadstick. Dad hands me my glass of water and waits for me to stop coughing. "Mom says you think it was your fault." I'm holding my breath. I don't know where this conversation is going. "It wasn't your fault, Georgia. And it wasn't Chester's fault either." I exhale so loudly, everyone in the restaurant must hear me.

"But you said Chester was the last straw. If I hadn't begged Mom to take me to the Humane Society, you never would have left home." My voice quivers.

"That isn't true, Georgia. Your mom and I weren't getting along. We were fighting almost every day. Remember a while back, I told you about a friend of mine, Erin, the anesthesiologist at the hospital?" How could I forget Erin, my dad's so-called *friend*? Erin the UGG-wearing doctor.

"What about her?" My voice is calm, as though my happiness doesn't depend on what Dad says next.

"Erin and I were seeing each other for a little while. It was more than a friendship. But we're not dating anymore. It's over."

"Why are you telling me this now? Does Mom know? Does this mean what I think it means?" I'm trying to be patient, but I have a million questions and I'm filled with real hope for the first time in a long time.

"Mom knows. I'm telling you now because I don't want you to think you or Chester had anything to do with me leaving. It was never about you." Chester was right. I never should have doubted his ability to predict the future about my parents' marriage. The outlook is good and getting better.

"So, you're coming home now, right?" My heart's beating faster.

"No. I'm not coming home, not now."

"But why not? Don't you still love Mom?" *Argh! What's wrong with me? I keep asking the wrong questions.*

"I do love her. It's complicated."

"Do you want to divorce her?" *When will I ever learn?* Emma says it's never a good idea to ask someone a question when in your heart, you know there can only be one answer you're willing to accept. And this time, the wrong answer is hanging from a thread. An image flashes in my brain of that poster you see everywhere, of a cat gripping a branch for dear life, screaming his head off. I am that cat, swallowing a silent scream as I wait for my dad to say something that will put me out of my misery.

"Being married to your mother isn't easy." Dad's fiddling with two breadsticks. I'm so mad I want to rip them out of his hands and smash them with my fists. "What can I say, Georgia? I always feel as though I have one foot on a skateboard, and the other foot's about to step on a banana peel."

I know my mom's not perfect, but *I'm* the only one allowed to criticize her. My father, *supposedly* an adult, a successful emergency room nurse, is sharing too much information. I don't need to know about Erin. I don't want to hear about how difficult it is for him to be married to my mom.

Then he tilts his head and smiles as though he's reading my mind. "I shouldn't be sharing all this with you. I'm sorry, Georgia. Maybe I should ask Chester for advice," he says.

I want to tell him I already asked Chester, and his prediction is Dad's coming home. But I'm not sure the time is right. The pizza arrives, and my dad changes the subject. He shares what he thinks are hilarious emergency room stories about the weird things little kids stuff up their noses. Those stories are not funny, if you ask me. And nothing my dad could possibly say would make me smile except "I'm coming home." Those are the magic words I'm waiting to hear.

We finish our pizza and talk about school and more adventures in the emergency room. I'm relieved to escape the conversation about my parents' marriage and the risky business of skateboards and banana peels. But my hope for a happy ending isn't totally squashed. And hope is something to hold onto.

Chapter 23
Assume Positive Intent

One block away from school on Thursday morning, I hear my name. "Georgia, wait up!" It's Reagan. She's running. She's out of breath. I spin around and wait, more out of curiosity than anything else.

"You are such a fast walker!" Reagan's panting as though she ran a marathon. "I've been trying to catch up to you since I saw you crossing Union Street." She's clutching her chest like she's about to pass out.

"What's up, Reagan?" I say. I turn back toward the school and start walking again, even faster than my usual pace. I have quite the mean streak when it comes to Reagan Worthington. Emma's been trying to get me to forgive her, to "assume positive intent," as her dad always tells her. But I think that's a fancy social worker phrase for pretending everyone is kind and no one wants to hurt you. I'm thinking "assuming positive intent" is an inherited trait, like eye color, and I don't have those genes.

"I wanted to tell you how much I loved your probability presentation. Your dog, Grandpa, is *soooooo* cute!"

"His name's Chester, not Grandpa."

"Oh right, Chester. He's *soooooo* smart!"

"Yeah, Chester's smart. He's a great dog," I say, stating the obvious.

"Listen, Georgia, the girls and I are having a movie night tomorrow at my house. Want to join us?"

"The girls?"

"Yeah, Marissa and Emma." Now Emma is one of Reagan's "girls." When did that become official? I'm not excited about the idea of spending my Friday night with Reagan and her main groupie, Marissa. On the other hand, Emma will be there, and I don't have other plans. I stop walking to give Reagan a chance to catch her breath again.

"What movie?" I ask, as though that matters.

"We haven't decided. You can choose. Just say you'll be there, okay? Six p.m. You'll come, right?" Why is Reagan so eager to hang out all of a sudden? Maybe Emma told her to invite me. It's not easy for me to give people like Reagan the benefit of the doubt. It's easy for people like Emma and her dad, and even my Aunt Felicia. She always assumes positive intent.

One time, we were driving on the highway, when another car cut my aunt off. "Someone must be about to have a baby! Hope they get to the hospital in time," she said. Aunt Felicia doesn't even criticize my dad. She assumes positive intent, like maybe my dad needs a break from the responsibility of marriage. It's a stretch. But thinking about Aunt Felicia pushes me to make a difficult decision. I will force myself to give it a try with Reagan. I'll assume positive intent. That will make Emma happy.

"Sure, I'll come," I agree. We reach the front entrance of the school, and we're about to go our separate ways when Reagan throws her arms around me for a hug.

She whispers in my ear. "Great! I'm so glad you're coming. And Georgia, bring Grandpa with you!" And then she's off, not even waiting for my reply. It isn't a question. It's an expectation. The truth is, Reagan could have been honest. She could have said, "If you want to hang out with me and the girls, then you better bring your smart, fortune-telling dog with you." And the worst part is, I don't even care. I'm excited about movie night with these girls. *What's wrong with me?*

• • •

I meet up with Emma in the cafeteria. We both brought our lunches, so we're the first kids at our favorite table next to the wall of windows. She's studying a slice of red pepper, lost in thought.

"Did you know Reagan invited me to movie night at her house?"

"I did know," Emma says. *That figures.*

"Did you tell Reagan to invite me? Was it your idea?"

"Stop it, Georgia. It was Reagan's idea. I told you. She likes you."

"Did she tell you she invited Chester, too?"

"She invited Chester? How sweet," Emma says.

"Hmm. We'll see." Now Emma's playing with her slice of red pepper, dunking it in and out of some greenish dip her mom packed for her. "Hey. Are you okay? You look tired."

"I think I'm coming down with something."

"Well you'd better show up for movie night at Reagan's house. Don't cancel on me, Emma. No way am I going there unless I know you're going. Promise me, you'll be there. Promise me you're going to movie night." She must hear the desperation in my voice.

"I promise, I promise." Our table fills up fast, it gets super noisy in the cafeteria, and I can hardly hear myself talk. By the time our lunch period is over, Emma's still playing with the same sliver of red pepper. *No wonder that girl's getting so skinny*, I think. And then I think, *She'd better be at Reagan's house for movie night.*

Chapter 24
Movie Night

Reagan opens her front door and gushes. "I'm so happy you came! And you brought your amazing dog!" Reagan's little brother, McKinley, also known as Mack, is playing a loud videogame in the family room, but when he sees Chester, he drops what he's doing and runs over to greet us.

"So, this is the famous dog, Grandma! Where are your teeth, Grandma?" Mack says.

"It's a boy, dummy. His name is Grandpa," Reagan snarls at her brother.

"His name is Chester," I say.

Reagan starts talking in that baby talk some people use whenever they talk to their pets. *What a good dog you are, aren't you? You're such a good dog.*" Chester sees right through the phony voice, although he puts on a good show, letting Reagan rub his belly. He's patient with annoying people, which is a trait he did *not* get from me.

"C'mon upstairs! Emma and Marisa are already here," Reagan says. Chester and I follow obediently.

The first thing I notice in Reagan's bedroom is the color of the walls. "Love the purple walls," I say.

"The paint color is actually called amethyst," she says in a *trying-too-hard-to-be-nice* tone of voice. "We're doing our nails. What color polish do you want?"

"Hi, Emma. Hi, Marisa," I say. Marisa is studying an enormous display of nail polishes arranged on Reagan's dresser. Emma is curled up on the rug, her arm cradling her head. Chester trots right over to her. He loves Emma.

"Hey, Georgia. Hey, Chester," Emma says, as she pulls herself to a sitting position. "What color does Chester want for his nails?" she asks, inspecting his paw.

"Oh, that's not going to happen," I say, before realizing Emma is only kidding about polishing Chester's nails. Marisa is holding a bottle of shimmery steel-grey polish. "That's a pretty color," I tell her. "Do you have any purple—I mean amethyst?" I ask. The words fly out before I realize how snarky they sound. Reagan keeps smiling. Either she's clueless or she's ignoring my sarcasm.

"Before we decide what color to choose for our nails, I have a great idea," Reagan says in a voice dripping with casualness, as though this whole scene hadn't been planned before I arrived. "Let's ask Chester and the Magic 8 Ball what color we should choose."

Dang! I wanted to assume positive intent, but deep down I suspected Reagan invited me because of Chester. She's using me for my psychic dog. She probably wants Chester to predict her future. She wants to know how many kids she's going to have, or where she'll go to college. "I didn't bring my Magic 8 Ball," I say. "Sorry. But I don't need Chester's advice. I think the amethyst polish will be perfect." Two can play this game of pretend.

"Not a problem," Reagan says. She opens the door to her closet. She reaches up for a shopping bag. "I just bought a Magic 8 Ball for Chester to use." She throws the bag on her bed, reaches in, and pulls out her new toy. It's cradled safely in a lot of packaging so it can't roll around. She opens the box. Chester tears himself away from cuddling-heaven with Emma and comes sniffing around. He's ready to play and ready for more attention.

The three girls sit down on the rug near Chester. They're ignoring me, as though this whole drama is somebody's idea of a new movie, *Mean Girls: Part II.* I glare at Emma. I thought she was above this kind of trick.

"Chester, should Georgia choose the amethyst nail polish?" Reagan asks. I can feel my face turn a shade that probably matches the walls. I want to grab that Magic 8 Ball out of her hand and throw it out the window. Chester sniffs the ball for a while. It must smell too new for him. I hope he refuses to cooperate, but he can't resist. He wants to play, and he wants to please. Chester rolls Reagan's Magic 8 Ball around the room. Then he sits back on his haunches, starts wagging his tail, and barks.

"Let me, let me," Marisa squeals. She leans over the ball and reads the words in the window. "*Outlook good.*"

"Yeah, I told you I didn't need Chester's advice," I say, rolling my eyes. This is so embarrassing. Why can't we watch a movie? Wasn't this supposed to be movie night? Emma's ignoring me. I'd like to know what she's thinking, but she's slumped down again, curled up on the rug with her head in her arms, totally checked out.

"Well, maybe nail polish color isn't something we need advice about, you're right, Georgia. But I could use advice about something that's way more important." Reagan's eyes fill up with tears, and her lower lip quivers. I wonder if Reagan's parents are getting a divorce. I wonder if her little brother is sick. I wonder if her dad lost his job, or if something tragic is going on in her life. I actually feel sorry for her.

"What's wrong, Reagan?" Emma asks, sitting up and suddenly paying attention.

"It's about the new kid, James, in seventh grade. I thought he liked me. And you know I've had a crush on him since he moved here in October. He used to be so friendly, and lately he doesn't even say hi. Maybe I should ask Chester if James still likes me." Is this why Reagan invited Chester and me over for movie night? To ask this pathetic question?

Anyone could understand why Reagan likes James. James O'Connor is taller than most of the other kids at our school. His eyes are dark blue, deep set, and he's always smiling. But not a goofy smile, more of a sly, sneaky smile—like he's thinking about something funny, but no one else is in on the joke.

I look over at Reagan. She has blue eyes too. I wonder about the odds of Reagan and James having blue-eyed children. After Elliott's presentation about eye color, she's probably wondering about the same thing. That's what happens when you're in Mr. Burnett's math class. You begin to see the world as one gigantic math problem.

"Well, let's ask Chester," Marisa says. Emma looks at me, waiting to see what I'll do. She's hugging her knees to her chest. Her sleeves are rolled up above her elbows. There are eggplant-colored bruises all over her arms. They look as though someone grabbed her hard. I wonder what happened, but I'm feeling so angry I don't even care. I look at Reagan. I look back at Marisa. I have no use for these girls. They are ganging up on me. Now even Emma's on their side.

"Seriously? Chester doesn't even know James." I try to reason with them.

"Well, your dog didn't know if the coins were heads or tails during your probability presentation, but he got it right every time with your Magic 8 Ball," Reagan says, in a sing-song voice. "Unless it was some trick. Was it all a trick, Georgia?" I'm cornered, and I know it.

"It wasn't a trick," I say. "Fine—ask Chester. But don't blame me if the answer isn't what you want to hear." I shrug one shoulder and sink my chin into my hand.

"Thank you, Georgia, you're the best! *Chester, come here, boy*!" Reagan calls him by his real name for once. She grips that Magic 8 Ball in her hands like it's made of solid gold. I push myself farther away from the circle, away from Reagan and Marisa, away from Emma. Away from these horrible girls who are using me for my psychic dog.

"You ask the question, Emma," Reagan says. "I'm too scared."

"Chester, does James like Reagan?" Emma asks so softly I can hardly hear her. Chester is ready. He moves the ball with his nose, rolls it around the floor a few times, and then stops it with his paw right in front of me, window side up. I look down at the words, and I feel a rush of joy. The same thrill you get when school's been canceled because of an unexpected snow storm.

"*Very doubtful*," I say with more than a hint of glee. "Sorry about that, Reagan." Reagan is silent at first, but I could cut the tension in the room with a butter knife. When she does speak, her voice slashes the silence with so much rage, I think I might be bleeding.

"What does your stupid, toothless dog know anyway?" Reagan says. Emma gasps. And then Reagan turns away from me. "Hey, Marisa, what movie should we watch tonight?" And just like that, I'm invisible again. Like magic.

I can't wait to get away from that house. We don't stay long enough to polish my nails amethyst or any other color. We don't stay long enough to watch the silly romantic comedy Reagan chooses. I would have picked *Mean Girls*, just to see them squirm. But no one asked me.

Chapter 25
Emma's Problem

It's the last day of this math unit, and there's a zero percent likelihood of anyone staying awake for one more presentation.

"Emma, welcome back! We've missed you," Mr. Burnett says. I haven't seen Emma since Friday night at Reagan's house. She's been absent for three days. I expected a phone call, a text, an apology, something, anything from my so-called best friend. But, not a word.

Even though I'm still angry, I do feel sorry for Emma. It's no fun being last. No one in this class wants to think about the chances of winning a baseball game or a measly dollar with a lottery ticket. No one wants to think about the likelihood of having blue eyes or the odds of having a marriage that lasts forever. We are one hundred percent bored out of our minds with the whole topic of probability and statistics.

"Emma, you are our last but definitely not our least presenter." Like most teachers, Mr. Burnett can be corny. Corniness must be something they make you learn at teachers' colleges.

Emma walks slowly to the back of the classroom, holding a rolled-up poster. She's wearing a black-and-white-striped sweatshirt that's way too big for her. Maybe it's the outfit, but Emma looks like a prisoner, dragging her feet, head down, miserable. She unrolls her poster and displays it on the bulletin board with the thumbtacks Mr. Burnett left on the ledge. She turns around, steps aside, and waits for the class's attention. She looks around the room, standing so tall and brave.

Marisa gasps. No one else makes a sound. My whole body freezes. I don't want Emma's problem. I want bags of stale M&M's from Halloween. I want Magic 8 Balls and board games with dice and colorful spinners. I want Emma to be okay. No one wants this. No one wants cancer.

WHAT ARE THE ODDS?

The odds of getting cancer: *Only 1 in 285 kids under 20 will get cancer. Lucky me.* ☺

The diagnosis: *I have Leukemia, a cancer of the blood.* ☹

The treatment: *Chemotherapy*

Probability Problem: *How can I increase my odds of beating cancer?*

Emma's voice is soft, but no one else is talking, so we can hear every word. We are trying to make sense of this horrible news. Even Matthew keeps his mouth shut for once.

"There's not much else I can tell you," Emma says. "Tomorrow, my parents are taking me to a children's hospital in Baltimore where I'm going to start treatment." I lean in so I can hear her better over the thrashing sound of my heartbeat. "Since we got the diagnosis, we've been doing research on the disease, what it means, and the best treatments available. We got a second opinion from a specialist in childhood cancers. We're optimistic that we're on the right track. But it's too early to predict."

Pinpricks of tears are stinging my eyes like angry little wasps. I remember the horrible bruises I saw on Emma's arms. I remember how tired she seemed, curled up on Reagan's carpet. I remember making her promise me she'd go to movie night. How could I have been so blind? Why didn't I see what was happening to Emma?

She looks at me, and I try to tell her with my eyes that I'm sorry. I'm sorry for being the worst friend in the universe. I'm sorry for being jealous of her friendship with Reagan. I'm sorry I didn't even ask about her bruises. I hope she can read my mind and she knows I care even though I've been a terrible human being.

Emma's voice is fading. "As for this probability problem, we can use all the support we can get, so… maybe you can help me increase my odds somehow. I don't know. But maybe." She nods her head at Mr. Burnett.

"Emma, thank you." Our teacher is holding his glasses in one hand, his shoulders are drooping, and his goofy smile has disappeared. "Thank you for sharing this information with us. I feel honored, and I think I speak for your classmates when I say we want to work on this problem with you. You are going to be busy for the next few days, weeks, maybe even months, fighting this disease. And we are also going to be busy, studying the different ways you can increase the probability for a full recovery."

Emma leaves the poster on the bulletin board and walks back to her desk. She gathers her books. She looks tired and pale. Her long-sleeved sweatshirt hides her bruises. "Thanks, Mr. Burnett. My mom's waiting for me in the office."

"Of course, Emma. We will be in touch." No one speaks. No one knows what to say. We watch her walk out the door, and I can't stop myself from wondering about the probability of seeing her again.

Chapter 26
My Sources Say I Hate You!

I let myself in the backdoor. My mom is in the kitchen. Why can't she be folding towels in the hallway or organizing shoes in her closet, anywhere besides the kitchen? I don't want to see her or talk to her. I'm not in the mood.

"Hey, honey, how was school?" Every day it's the same question: *How was school? How was school? How was school?* Can't she come up with something different for a change?

I could say, "Fine," to get her off my back. I could ignore her. But heck, my mom wants to know how school was today, so I'll tell her. It's her own fault for asking.

"How was school? You really want to know?" I'm raising my voice, and I'm only getting started. My mom stops chopping green peppers and looks up from her cutting board. "School was terrible. It was the worst day of school I've ever had in my life!"

I take a deep breath, and then I blurt out the cruel words that make no sense. "Emma has cancer!"

"Oh, Georgia, no—that's terrible. What kind of cancer?" *What kind of cancer?* I can't believe that's all she wants to know. Of all the heartless questions in the world, this one is the most cold-blooded she could have asked, and that question unleashes the rage inside me like an erupting volcano. And I don't mean the sort of volcano kids make for science projects with baking soda and vinegar. I hold nothing back, my voice cracks, and I spew red hot lava, destroying everything in my path. I don't care who gets hurt. In fact, I *want* someone to hurt, at least as much as I'm hurting.

"What kind of cancer? What difference does it make? Emma has cancer. Kids aren't supposed to get cancer. How would you feel if I had cancer? Would that make you happy? I hate you! I hate you so much!" I'm screaming at the top of my lungs.

Chester cowers under the kitchen table. Poor Chester. He's never heard me scream like this before. Neither has my mom. I throw my backpack across the kitchen floor and stomp down the hall to my bedroom. I slam my door, but I'm just warming up. I pick up my Magic 8 Ball and throw it hard enough to make a dent in the drywall above my desk. I don't throw it hard enough to crack the plastic shell surrounding all the answers I need and

all the answers I dread. That thing must be made of steel. I crawl into bed and cover my shaking body with my comforter. I close my eyes and decide I am not leaving my bedroom again for the rest of my life.

Chapter 27
Doug's Doggie Bowls

Things are happening too fast. All I want to do is hide under my covers and wait for the good news that Emma has beaten cancer. But the universe has other ideas, and hiding is not an option for me.

After my coin-toss presentation, stories about Chester spread through the school like poison ivy on a Girl Scout. Then, a few days after we learn Emma has cancer, the Doug's Mugs commercial airs on TV, and *everyone* is talking about Chester and the Magic 8 Ball. All this excitement should distract me from worrying about my friend and about my parents' marriage. But I'm having trouble sleeping through the night. Although he's trying, even Chester can't stop my worrying.

My cousin Sam convinces me to let Chester make an appearance at my uncle's coffee shop on Saturday afternoon. "Trust me, Georgia. Business has been great since the TV commercials, and this will make Chester even more famous." I'm not convinced Chester's fame will persuade my dad to come home. But Sam seems to think it will help. "It's worth a try," she says.

Dad drops Chester and me off in front of the coffee shop. A long line of customers snakes around the corner. Before I shut the car door, my dad reminds me, "Mom will pick you up in two hours." Then he pulls away from the curb, leaving us on our own.

People standing outside the front door of Doug's Mugs are pointing at us. Then someone in the crowd squeals, "There he is! There's Chester!"

A police officer standing near the entrance of the coffee shop waves his own Magic 8 Ball in the air. "I have a question, over here, one question, please!" he shouts. Then two teenage girls try to take selfies with poor Chester. I search for an escape route. Eventually the crowd parts to let us by. We walk through the door of Doug's Mugs Coffee Shop, Chester leading the way, pulling at the end of his leash.

When he sees us, Uncle Doug sprints from the back of the shop. His eyes are sparkling, he's bouncing from one foot to the other, and he tries to fist-bump me. How can anyone be this happy when my friend has cancer?

All I can think about is Emma. Has she started her treatments? How is she feeling? Will she be okay? How can I improve her odds of beating cancer? I want to be home at my computer, researching Emma's disease and figuring out how to help her destroy this uninvited monster who crept into her life. Instead, I'm here at my uncle's coffee shop, helping to make Chester famous so the shop gets more business and my dad moves back home. None of this makes sense anymore.

"Chester, Georgia, come right this way, we have a special table for the two of you." Uncle Doug has set up a corded-off area in the back. He's placed a mat on the floor for Chester, and there's a brand-new Magic 8 Ball on the table. I look up and read the enormous sign posted on the wall:

ASK CHESTER
Doug's Mugs, the best coffee in the world!
You can count on it!

"Ask Chester? What does that mean, Uncle Doug?"

"Here's the plan, Georgia. When customers buy a drink and purchase a mug, they get to ask Chester one question."

"What? You never told me that part of your plan. I thought we were here to greet customers and drink hot chocolate."

"One question for each mug purchased, and of course you can have all the hot chocolate you can drink." I put my hand on my hip and tap my foot, the closest I can get in public to letting him know I'm furious. "Don't be nervous, Georgia. It will be fun, and did you see the line outside? Business has never been this good."

Uncle Doug ignores me. He squats next to Chester as though my opinion of the "Ask Chester" plan doesn't count. "Good boy, Chester. Good boy! Yes, you are," Uncle Doug says with his lovey-dovey voice. "We may even run out of mugs today thanks to you, Chester!" Then he remembers I'm still there and goes back to using his Uncle Doug voice. "Georgia, how about a large hot chocolate with plenty of whipped cream? And Chester, you get a special bowl of water. Make yourselves comfortable, you two." And with that, Uncle Doug dashes off, leaving Chester and me to settle in.

As we wait for our drinks, poor Chester is quivering all over, and his sad eyes tell me he's as unhappy about the situation as I am. There's too much noise in the coffee shop and too many people. The coffee bean grinder sounds like a summer hailstorm, and customers are shouting out their orders to be heard over the deafening roar of the milk steamer. The whole shop smells skunky with the scent of strong coffee. No wonder Chester's freaking out. Everyone's staring at him, and he's not used to the attention. And how is Chester supposed to answer strangers' questions and predict their futures with a Magic 8 Ball? What if he gives them answers they don't want? And how does this plan help me get my dad to move back home? I understand how this will help Uncle Doug, but Sam promised the plan would fix both of our families' problems.

As I'm trying to keep Chester calm, my cousin brings the hot chocolate over to our back table. Uncle Doug used my favorite mug. It has a silvery-blue glaze, and it's extra tall. Whipped cream swirls inches above the rim, looking like an iceberg, and Uncle Doug sifted some cocoa powder on top. It's still too hot to drink, even with the cold whipped cream melting into the chocolate sea below. It will take more than a mug of hot chocolate with whipped cream to convince me this whole *Ask Chester* plan is a good idea.

"Don't be too mad at my dad," Sam says, sitting next to me. The truth is, I'm angry with Sam, too. It was her idea to include Chester and the Magic 8 Ball in Uncle Doug's advertising campaign.

"I haven't seen Dad this excited for years. I think Chester has given him a reason to create more pottery, to get back to his art, his true passion in life," Sam says. "Here comes Chester's new bowl! You are going to love it, Georgia."

Uncle Doug places a large bowl of water in front of Chester. "Did Sam tell you I've started making pet pottery? Food and water bowls for dogs and cats, Georgia." We watch Chester lap up the water with gusto, splashing more liquid onto the rubber mat than he manages to lap into his toothless mouth. The bowl has his name carved into the side in fancy cursive letters. I have to admit it's beautiful. Uncle Doug placed paw print indentations around the outside rim. The letters and paw prints are shiny black, and he used a dark-red glaze with coppery sparkles. It's a work of art. It's a masterpiece, and my uncle is beaming with pride.

Uncle Doug leans over and whispers, "Is Chester ready for his first customer?" What am I supposed to say? I tell myself not only will we be helping to improve business in the coffee shop, but we're supporting my uncle's passion for pottery. Sam's right. I haven't seen him this happy in a long time. I can't disappoint him. Chester and I are stuck, and we all know it.

"Chester's ready," I say, taking a deep breath. "And I guess I'm as ready as I'll ever be."

Chapter 28
Ask Again Later

A silver-haired man hobbles over to the table with a large mug in one hand, a cane in the other. He sits in the chair across from me and sighs deeply. I'm not at all prepared for this, but I dive in with introductions. "Hi, my name is Georgia, and this is my dog, Chester. Do you have a question for the Magic 8 Ball?" Sam's hovering a few feet away from us, wiping down the already clean tables and chairs.

"My name is Mr. Brody. Abe Brody. And yes, I do have a question." The man pats Chester on the head a few times. Chester gazes at him with his big brown eyes and a face filled with love. Then he places his sweet head on the man's leg.

"What's your question, Mr. Brody?" I ask, picking up the Magic 8 Ball.

"My wife passed away last year, and I've been living by myself. It's hard for me to get around since the hip surgery. My daughter and son-in-law want me to move in with them. But I don't want to leave my home. I'm happy where I am. Does Chester think I should move?"

I can't imagine Chester has an opinion about whether Mr. Brody should move in with his daughter and son-in-law. I don't think this important decision should be up to a silly Magic 8 Ball and a dog, even a dog as smart as Chester. But what am I supposed to do?

"Well let's see what the Magic 8 Ball tells us," I say. This customer bought a mug, and he expects something besides the best coffee in the universe in return for his purchase. He expects an answer. I place the Magic 8 Ball on the floor in front of Chester. "Should Mr. Brody move in with his daughter?"

We watch Chester roll the Magic 8 Ball around on the floor next to his mat. He barks as soon as the ball rolls to a stop. I lift it gently from the floor and present it to Mr. Brody with the window facing up. The man pulls out a pair of glasses from his vest pocket, looks down at the words appearing in the window and reads the message aloud.

"It says, *Ask again later*." I worry this vague response means the man will think he can come back later in the afternoon so he can ask again. I should have worked out the details with my uncle, but there wasn't time to consider all the what-ifs.

A wide grin spreads across Mr. Brody's face. The wrinkles around his twinkling eyes grow deeper.

"Well, that's a relief. It seems Chester agrees with me. Now is not the right time to make the move. I'll ask again later. Maybe next year. We'll see how things go. Thank you, Chester, and thank you, Georgia." I notice a hop in his step as he leaves the coffee shop without even using his cane.

Sam saunters over to my table and gives me a quick hug. "I don't think you need me hanging around. You and Chester are doing fine," she says. "I'm going to help fill the coffee orders. I'll check in later." I appreciate the compliment, but I'm still mad at Sam for not warning me about this plan. I let her hug me, but I don't hug back. I know she'll get the message she is *not* forgiven. Not yet.

Next up is a teenage girl about Sam's age. "I need some advice from your dog," she says, clutching her new mug. "I don't know where I should go to college next year. My boyfriend wants me to go to his university in Wisconsin, so we can live near each other. But I want to go to Yale. What should I do?" For someone who got into one of the best universities in the country, the question is stupid. Then I remember what Mr. Burnett always says: *There are no stupid questions.*

"'What should I do?' is not the right kind of question," I say. "You need to ask Chester a yes-no question. How about this: Should I go to Yale next year?"

"Perfect! Should I go to Yale, Chester?" I place the Magic 8 Ball on the floor, and Chester knows what to do. The girl is thrilled to read the answer: "*Without a doubt.*" She leans over to give me a huge hug. "Thank you so much! I feel better already." It's actually fun making people happy, giving them answers they want.

Chapter 29
The Answers They Were Looking For

We're speeding through one customer after another. It doesn't take long to discover it's impossible to make everyone happy. But when customers get answers they don't want, I tell them they should follow their hearts. After all, Chester is smart, but he isn't perfect. And when we give customers the answers they want, I feel almost as joyful as they feel. Chester's happy either way. He's adjusted to the coffee shop sounds and smells, and he's enjoying all the friendly people.

A young couple sits down at the table with matching mugs of steaming tea. "Hi, I'm Georgia, and this is Chester."

"Well, this is embarrassing," the young man says. "I'm Rob, and this is my girlfriend, Laura." The two look at each other. I wait for their question.

The woman shrugs her shoulders and says, "What do we have to lose?" I'm thinking: *Maybe you have nothing to lose. Maybe you have everything to lose. And maybe you shouldn't be asking a dog with a Magic 8 Ball an embarrassing question.* But I keep my snarky thoughts to myself.

"Rob and I are thinking about getting married, but we're not sure. So many couples we know are getting divorced. My own parents got divorced when I was a kid," Laura says.

I'm wondering if I should tell them about their chances. I'm wondering if I should ask them if they have college degrees or if they're older than twenty-two. I'm wondering if the odds are in this couple's favor. But mostly I'm feeling the weight of their future digging into my shoulders like a four-hundred-pound backpack.

"Chester," Rob says, scratching my dog behind the ears, "Should Laura and I tie the knot? What do you think?" I place the Magic 8 Ball on the floor. Before Chester has time to get his paws on it, I change my mind. I scoop that Magic 8 Ball off the floor. I take a deep breath, and then I take a chance.

"Listen, maybe this is none of my business," I say. "But do you really want your future decided by a dog and a Magic 8 Ball?" Laura and Rob look at each other.

"Laura, what do you think?" Rob asks.

"I don't know what to do," she says.

"Well, what do you hope the Magic 8 Ball's answer will be?" I ask. *Since when did I get so smart?*

"What do I hope? I hope the answer is *yes, without a doubt,*" Rob says, laughing.

"I hope the answer is *all signs point to definitely marry that man*!" Laura says.

"Well, there's your answer. You don't really have a question for Chester today. But you have some beautiful mugs. I hope that's enough." My Uncle Doug won't be happy if they return those mugs because they didn't get an answer from Chester.

Rob and Laura gaze at each other with so much love in their eyes. I wonder if my parents ever looked at each other that way. The happy couple thanks me—a clueless twelve-year-old middle school kid. They stroll away arm in arm with their new mugs and the answer they wanted. It's the answer they already had in their hearts.

And then, life gets even stranger. One of our last customers of the day sits down at my table. The boy's wearing a baseball cap that's too big for him, and it's pulled down low, masking his face in a dark shadow. He's thin. He slouches down in the chair, and his limbs are spindly like a daddy longlegs spider. Before I have a chance to make introductions, he starts to talk.

"My mom doesn't know I'm here. She'd kill me if she knew, which is actually ironic because I'm probably going to die soon anyway." His skin is pasty. His cheeks are hollow. He has no eyebrows, no eyelashes, and I know why this boy is here. I want to grab Chester and run out of Doug's Mugs Coffee Shop and keep running. But I can't move. I'm holding my breath, waiting for this boy to tell me what I already know but don't want to hear.

"I'm sick," he says. For some reason, I lean away from him. I'm not even thinking. "Don't worry it's not contagious. It's a rare disease. You've never heard of it. No one's ever heard of it."

"Cancer?" I whisper.

"No. I wish I had cancer. Then I'd have some hope. I have a genetic disorder. Most people who have my disease don't make it to their early twenties." I don't know what to say to him. *I'm sorry* feels like the wrong thing. And so, I say the only thing I can think of.

"Do you have a question?"

"All I want to know is if I'm going to make it to my eighteenth birthday in a few months," he says. "That's my question."

My heart sinks. Chester and my Magic 8 Ball must give this kid a positive answer. The answer has to be *Yes, Without a doubt, You may rely on it. Yes, definitely*. Of course, you'll make it to your eighteenth birthday. There can be no other answer. And yet, with only ten possible positive answers in the Magic 8 Ball, I know we have only a fifty-fifty chance of something close to hope. I place that Magic 8 Ball on the floor, and I hold my breath.

I'm trying to send Chester a message with my silent thoughts. Maybe he can sense how desperate I am, how desperate this boy must be. Instead of rolling the ball around, Chester puts his adorable snout on the boy's leg, giving me a chance to breathe, a chance to think.

"My name's Georgia, and the dog drooling all over your jeans is Chester," I say. The boy laughs.

"I'm Tom." He's petting Chester's head. Chester closes his eyes, and he's acting as though he's having the most glorious moment of his life. His tongue is hanging out a mile, and he looks silly. Tom laughs again. "I like your dog," he says. We sit quietly, not talking, as Tom gives Chester all of his attention and lots of love.

It's a moment in time. Quiet and peaceful. Nothing else matters. All the things in the world that have happened before this moment and all the things that will happen after this moment melt away like the whipped cream in my mug of hot chocolate. I know the whipped cream is there. I can't see it, and yet it makes the hot chocolate even sweeter.

Finally, Tom breaks the silence. "Listen, I changed my mind. I'm going to take back my question." Tom picks up the Magic 8 Ball from

Chester's mat and hands it to me. "It was nice meeting you two, and hey, I love my new mug," he says. Tom shakes Chester's paw before he strolls away.

Chapter 30
Suede Boots

By the time Uncle Doug runs out of mugs, I'm feeling sick to my stomach from drinking too many hot chocolates. Chester needs a walk. My mom should be here, but she's running late. We walk to the counter, and when I'm about to ask Sam if she'll take us home, she peers over my head and starts waving to someone at the front door.

I turn around and see my dad walking into the coffee shop. He's with someone I don't know. She's wearing black suede boots, a black skirt, a colorful blouse with pictures of birds and plants all over it, and she has long curly hair. Who is this woman chatting and laughing with my dad? Finally, Dad sees me standing at the counter, and they walk over.

"Hi, Dad," I say.

"Hey, Georgia. Hey, Last Straw." He bends down to pet Chester, then turns toward the woman next to him. "Erin, this is Georgia. Georgia, meet Erin," he says. And suddenly I feel like I'm going to barf all over the floor of Doug's Mugs Coffee Shop.

I ignore Erin's outstretched hand. "Where's Mom?" I ask. "She was supposed to pick me up twenty minutes ago." The veins in my forehead are pulsing, and my voice is quivering. I'd convinced myself Dad was getting ready to come home. How could I have been so blind?

I glare at my dad, ignoring the woman by his side. He's stuffing his hands in his pockets, like a guilty kid who broke a window with a baseball. He's shifting his weight from one foot to the other. He's shrugging his shoulders and tilting his head, trying to act charming.

"Your mom called me earlier, said she was running late. She asked me to pick you up. So… here we are."

"Hi, Georgia. I've heard so much about you," Erin says. She's given up on shaking my hand. She smiles. Her too-white teeth light up the coffee shop like an annoying fluorescent bulb. I don't return the smile. I don't want Erin in my life. I don't want Erin in my father's life. I want to go home.

"Hi," I croak. I stare daggers at my father. "Chester needs a walk. Will you take us home? Now?" If my mom heard my tone of voice, she would say, "Stop being rude and lose the surly attitude." Or maybe she'd be happy and proud of me for giving my dad's "friend" the cold shoulder.

I clip Chester's leash to his collar, and I grab his beautiful new bowl, the one Uncle Doug made for him. I'm in a hurry, so I don't notice the three inches of water in the bottom of his bowl. I splash the stream of water from his bowl all over Erin's suede boots. *Oops!*

"Oh dear," Erin gasps in horror—as though water on suede boots is worse than your parents getting a divorce, worse than cancer. Chester and I march out the door of Doug's Mugs without even saying sorry. After all, it's only a little water. I could have barfed all over those fancy designer boots. Erin should consider herself lucky.

Chapter 31
The Very Last Straw

I'm wide awake. It's the middle of the night, and Chester is snoozing on his blanket in the corner of my room. I roll out of bed and wake him up, patting the floor next to him. "Chester, come here, boy." It takes a minute, but Chester opens one eye, then another. I scratch behind his ears. "Wake up, Chester," I whisper. He stretches his forelegs in front of him then his back legs behind him. He sticks his butt up in the air as though he's doing a yoga pose. Finally, he starts licking my hand.

I grab my Magic 8 Ball, determined to give Chester a chance to make things right. I need to be as direct as I can be. I whisper my question into the darkness. "Will my parents get a divorce?"

I'd avoided that question for too long. I'd asked Chester if my dad hated my mom more than he loved me. I'd asked Chester if everything was going to work out. But those questions were the wrong questions. What does it even mean for everything to work out? Work out for my mom? For my dad? For my dad's girlfriend? Maybe Chester and the Magic 8 Ball didn't understand the questions. This time, I need a real answer, so I need to ask the right question. I need to know the future. And I think I'm ready.

I place the Magic 8 Ball on the floor next to Chester and whisper the words again, this time under his floppy ear. "Will my parents get a divorce?" Chester tilts his head, refusing to cooperate. "Come on, Chester, you spent the day answering questions for total strangers in Uncle Doug's coffee shop. This question is for us. It's important. It's about our family, our future!" I beg. "Will Mom and Dad get a divorce? *Yes* or *No*? *Without a doubt* or *Very doubtful*? *Outlook good* or *Outlook not so good*? *My reply is yes* or *My reply is no*?"

Everyone knows dogs can hear and smell better than humans. They can hear fear and joy, they can smell disgust and sorrow. I even read trained dogs can detect if someone has cancer, even before a doctor's diagnosis. If dogs can smell cancer, there's a good chance Chester can smell my desperation.

I wait. Nothing. Maybe Chester is too sleepy. Maybe he doesn't know the answer. Maybe he doesn't want to upset me. He curls up on my lap and closes his eyes. I guess I'll give up on my parents' marriage for now. I'll ask again tomorrow. But then, another desperate question floats into my tired brain. It's a different question, one I've been too terrified to ask before this moment.

Thinking about how some dogs can detect cancer made me think about Emma. And one thought led to another, which led to an even more important question. I nudge Chester off my lap, and I look him right in his sleepy eyes. "This is serious, Chester," I say. I take a deep breath. "Is Emma going to be okay?" I only have to ask once.

Chester places his paw on the Magic 8 Ball. He pushes it back and forth, back and forth, around in a circle, and we watch as it rolls to a stop under my desk. I scoot over to read the message floating in a sea of bluish ink, and it's not the answer I want. Not even close.

Don't count on it. WHAT? How can this be the answer? Don't count on it? Don't count on Emma being okay? Chester must sense my rage. He skulks back to the corner of my room.

I grab that stupid toy, pull up the screen of my bedroom window, and I gaze at the driveway hugging the side of our house. The streetlights are close and bright, and I can see every crack in the asphalt. I hold my useless Magic 8 Ball over my head with both hands and throw it out my window with so much force it cracks against the hard pavement. It bounces a few times and splatters the surface with inky blue dye. The moonlit canvas of our driveway looks like the beginning of an abstract painting, like something Jackson Pollock might have created. The probability for my Magic 8 Ball's survival is not good. As a matter of fact, all signs point to never again. And that outlook will have to be fine. I'm done with magic. There has to be another way.

Chapter 32
Helping Emma

Finally, some good news. Reagan and I got emails from Emma! She's still in Baltimore. Her parents are flying back and forth, taking turns being with her in the hospital and staying with her little brother at home. She tells us the chemotherapy has made her feel horrible, she's lost more weight and hair, but the doctors are optimistic that the treatment is working. She still has a long road ahead of her. Reagan and I tell Mr. Burnett it's time for our class to get busy. We promised to help increase the odds for Emma's full recovery.

"So, people, we're going to take a break from geometry for a few days. We promised Emma we would work on her very important problem," Mr. Burnett says. Reagan's hand shoots up in the air. "Yes, Reagan."

"I've been thinking about how we can help Emma. And I have a great idea." Reagan doesn't say she has *an idea* like most people would say. She says she has a *great idea.* That's because Reagan Worthington is the least humble person in the universe.

"That's wonderful, Reagan," Mr. Burnett says. Lucky for Reagan, our teacher is the most patient person in the universe. "Before you share your idea, we're going to take some time to think more about the problem. I'd like you to work on this with your math partners today. I'll give you time to brainstorm, and then we'll have an opportunity to share." Reagan's smug smile fades a bit. She'll have to wait to share her "great idea."

As Mr. Burnett distributes black magic markers and large sheets of chart paper, he announces our new math partnerships for the month of May. Although Elliott is now stuck with Matthew, I notice a thick library book about astrophysics half-hidden in his desk. Poor Matthew is on his own.

When Mr. Burnett announces my new partner, my jaw drops. "Georgia, you'll work with Reagan this month." I can't believe what I'm hearing. How could Mr. Burnett do this to me? I don't hear the rest of his directions, but everyone starts to move and talk at the same time, and the room gets so noisy I can't think. Reagan plunks down next to me and picks up the marker as though she's in charge.

"Do you have any ideas?" Reagan asks. I'd love to grab that black magic marker right out of her hand, but I control myself.

"It's not like we're scientists who can discover a cure for cancer in time to help Emma. What's your *great* idea?" I don't even try to control the sarcasm.

"I was thinking we could have a bake sale to raise money for cancer research." Reagan's "great" idea is so lame. A bake sale? We'd probably raise a few hundred dollars. You need more than a few hundred dollars to cure cancer. I can feel my eyes rolling to the back of my head, but I actually count all the way to ten in my brain, and I keep my mouth shut. Reagan writes the words BAKE SALE on our chart.

"I've been sending her cards and letters," I say. "But maybe the whole class could send jokes and funny stories to make her laugh. You know what they say, *laughter is the best medicine.*" It's another pathetic idea, but I can't think of anything else.

"That's a fantastic idea," Reagan says. She's so encouraging. I feel guilty I thought her idea was lame. She writes SEND JOKES TO MAKE EMMA LAUGH.

And then Reagan asks me a dangerous question. I should have expected it. I'm not prepared with an answer, but I should have known someone would ask. Leave it to Reagan to be the one.

"I probably shouldn't ask you this… but I can't stop thinking about it. Georgia, have you used the Magic 8 Ball with Chester to find out if Emma's going to get well?" She must see something that scares her when she looks into my eyes. "Never mind. I don't want to know. Pretend I didn't ask that question." And then Reagan puts her head down on the desk, hiding her face in her arms. Her body heaves like she's sobbing, but it's a silent sobbing, not the kind to get attention. I put my hand on her shoulder, to let her know I'm there. And I understand. And maybe, I want her to know we're all in this together.

• • •

On the way home from school that day, I keep thinking about Chester and Emma. I do my best thinking when I'm walking alone.

Questions and thoughts are swirling around in my brain leading me from one idea to another. It's as though I'm leaping from rock to rock, trying to cross a raging river. First, I'm thinking: *Why did Reagan change her mind about wanting to know about Emma's future?* Next, I'm thinking: *What about Tom, the boy we met at Doug's Mugs Coffee Shop who asked whether he'd make it to his eighteenth birthday? What was it about being with Chester that made him change his mind about wanting to know the answer?* Then, I'm thinking: *There must be some way Chester and I can help Emma increase the odds for her recovery. There has to be a way that has nothing to do with a Magic 8 Ball.*

And rock by rock, all of these questions and thoughts lead me to the other side of the river. I have an idea. I can't say it's a great idea, the way Reagan would say. For now, it's only a few pieces of a jigsaw puzzle for the bigger picture I have in my brain. Even though I'm on the other side of the river, I have hurdles to overcome on this journey. But at least I know what I need to do. I have my work cut out for me, and deep down, I know I'm up to the task.

I spend every spare minute of every day that week, researching, investigating, studying, learning, and finally, most of the puzzle pieces are in place. I know exactly what I'm going to do. Finally, I have a real plan that has nothing to do with magic, and everything to do with me. A plan that could truly make a difference.

Chapter 33
Permission

Even though I'm focused on helping Emma, I still haven't given up on my parents' marriage. Not even close. I'm moving forward with my plan, and it's right on schedule. My next move requires finding a way to put Mom and Dad in the same place at the same time. And since I need their support for my project to help Emma, I have the perfect excuse.

The place will be a table at Roberto's Pizza. The time will be Wednesday night at six p.m. That's when I'll ask for their permission to move forward with my Help Emma Project.

I call Dad while Mom's busy making dinner. "Dad, I need to talk to you and Mom about something important. Just the two of you, alone. Can I invite Mom to our Wednesday night dinner this week?"

"Of course. What's wrong, Georgia? Is everything okay?" Dad's concerned, and that's exactly what I want. When he finds out why I want to meet with both of them together, he'll be so relieved I'm not in any kind of trouble, he'll give me anything I want. I'm setting him up for a "yes," and he doesn't have a clue.

"I'm okay. We'll talk more Wednesday. Bye, Dad."

And then I ask my mom the next morning after breakfast. "Mom, what are you doing Wednesday night?"

"Dinner with Aunt Felicia, why?"

"I need to talk to you and Dad about something important. Just the two of you, alone. Can you come to Roberto's Pizza with us? Dad already said it was fine with him."

"Of course. I'll cancel dinner with Aunt Felicia. What's wrong, Georgia? Is everything okay?" Despite the fact they can't agree about much of anything, my parents are so much alike it's scary.

     •   •   •

It's Wednesday night, and my dad is already at Roberto's waiting for us in our favorite booth. I slide into the seat across from him, not leaving enough room next to me for my mom. I'm hoping she'll take the hint and sit next to Dad. Unfortunately, that part of my plan fails. My mom practically sits on top of me and shoves me closer to the wall. "Move over, Georgia. Hi, George," she says.

"Carrie Ann, good to see you." So, here we are, a family again. Sitting in our favorite booth at Roberto's Pizza. My cheeks hurt from grinning.

"Good to see you, too, George." My parents are friendly enough, but they both seem miserable. The moment reminds me of how I feel when I get to the end of a great book—it's the last page, and I've loved that book. Now that it's over, I'm sad because there are no more pages to turn. Even happy books have endings.

We order dinner, and it's obvious by their worried faces my parents are nervous about why I set up this family meeting. "What's up, Georgia?" my dad says. "You have us both a little anxious."

"I've made a decision about something important," I say. "I need your help." I fill them in about how our math class is going to have a bake sale and donate the money to cancer research, and how we're all going to collect jokes and send them to Emma because laughter is the best medicine.

"We're going to make a music video for her, too, and put it on YouTube." Turns out, that was Reagan's "great idea." She didn't write it on our chart, because she wanted to make a big announcement in front of the class. She wanted everyone to know it was her suggestion and I had nothing to do with it. I hate to admit it, but making a music video is a great idea, especially since

Reagan's cousin is a dance teacher and promises to choreograph the whole thing.

"But I want to do more to help Emma," I say. "I did some research and came up with a plan. I think it can make a difference. But I can't take the next step unless I have your permission."

"What do you have in mind, Georgia?" my mom asks. That's when the pizzas and salads arrive. I take a deep breath and wait for our server to move on to another table.

"I want to register Chester and me for pet therapy training. I'm under eighteen, so I need your permission, and a parent has to go with us to the training. I know how busy you both are, but a parent has to be there with us when we volunteer." They both sigh with relief. I wonder what they imagined. They always think the worst.

"I think we need a little more information about this," my mom says.

I tell them about my research and the studies that prove pet therapy has a positive effect on cancer patients, especially pediatric patients. "Pet therapy even decreases patients' pain levels and increases their optimism," I say. "I think Chester has the perfect personality for this. In fact, I think Chester has a gift for this kind of volunteer work."

"I've read some of those studies," my dad says. "I've seen pet therapy teams on some of the wards at the hospital. The pets and their handlers wear special vests, so I assume the hospital has programs in place to provide the service."

My mom's getting emotional. Almost crying. "Honey, it sounds like a wonderful idea. And you and Chester would be a terrific team. You're both loving, and kind, and smart, too!"

"That's true," my dad says. "And between Chester and Georgia, at least one member of this pet therapy team is actually obedient—maybe one is enough!" *Ha, ha. Not the least bit funny.* I force myself to laugh along with my parents. It's been a while since I've heard them laughing together. The least I can do is join in.

"What's next?" my mom asks. She's smiling.

"I'll complete the online registration, and all I need is one or both of you to agree to participate with Chester and me." I'm holding my breath, waiting for one of my parents to say something. I don't have to hold my breath for very long, thank goodness, because they say the same thing at the same time.

"I'll do it!" they say, as if they've rehearsed. I wait for one of my parents to back out.

"I'd really like to do this with Georgia," my dad says.

"I'd really like to do this with Georgia, too." My parents are glaring at each other like they're having a staring contest. I wonder who's going to look away first. I can't believe they're going to argue about who gets to go to pet therapy training with me. *What have I done?*

"Should I sign you *both* up for the training?" I'm braiding and unbraiding my hair, worrying about how this latest feud is going to end.

"Why not? Let's both do it!" my mom says. I squeeze her hand under the table. She's miserable about what's happening to our family, and like in the nursery rhyme about Humpty Dumpty, she wants to put our family back together again. I don't think that particular nursery rhyme ended happily, but I'm holding out hope for our family.

"Great idea. We'll both go with you, Georgia," Dad says. "Find out when the training will be. And if you let me know in advance, I'll arrange my schedule to be available." He's smiling, too. "And I have a joke you might want to send to Emma to help her recover. Want to hear it?"

I don't want to hear it. My dad's jokes are lame. But I need to reward him for agreeing to join Mom and me for pet therapy training. "Sure, Dad. What's your joke?"

"Knock, knock."

"Who's there?" I've never liked knock-knock jokes. They're so preschool.

"Pizza," he says as he finishes off the last slice of pepperoni and double cheese.

"Pizza who?"

"Pizza terrific guy."

"That's such a bad joke, Dad," I say.

"That's about the worst knock-knock joke I've ever heard," my mom says.

"Tell me how you really feel." My dad's scowling. "Do you have a better one?" Oh geez, now they're fighting over knock-knock jokes.

"No more knock-knock jokes, *please*," I beg.

"Fine," my mom says, finishing off her kale salad, not smiling anymore. My dad asks for the check, rolling his eyes at my mom, clearly annoyed. And I think to myself, *Adults fight about the weirdest things.*

Chapter 34
Math Humor

Mr. Burnett is an amazing math teacher, but he could never be a stand-up comic.

"Okay, people," he says. "Take out your math journals and work on this problem." I'm expecting another perimeter and area problem for his asymmetrical vegetable garden or his five-sided dog pen.

"How do you make seven even?" He writes the math problem on the board. Then he turns around, business as usual, and says, "Do the math!"

"Subtract one," Matthew calls out. This is when Mr. Burnett is supposed to frown at Matthew and remind him that when he says "do the math," we're expected to work with our math partners.

Instead, our teacher shakes his head and says, "No, Matthew. The only way to make seven even is to subtract the S." He waits for us to laugh. We don't laugh. "Don't you get it? It's a joke. Take the *S* away from the word *seven*, and you're left with the word *even*." Mr. Burnett punctuates his explanation by circling the "S" in the word "seven" on the board and then underlining the word "even." It's a silly riddle. It's a third-grader-might-think-that's-cute-but-probably-won't-laugh kind of riddle. Poor Mr. Burnett may have told the most cringeworthy joke of his life. Worse than my dad's knock-knock jokes. Then Reagan raises her hand. "Yes, Reagan."

She speaks slowly, her voice dripping with phony patience, as if she doesn't want to hurt our teacher's feelings. "Mr. Burnett, we know you're trying, but really, that wasn't a funny joke. I have a suggestion." I give her credit for telling a teacher he's not funny right to his face and in front of the whole class. That may not have been smart, but it took courage. Mr. Burnett earns my respect for not acting offended. He reacts like the cool teacher he is. He shrugs it off, as though he's used to people not laughing at his jokes.

"Okay, it was a stupid joke," he admits. "And Reagan, I would love to hear any suggestion you may have to improve my joke-telling skills. Mrs. Burnett will thank you."

"You always tell us there are no stupid questions and maybe there are no stupid jokes. But if we're going to help Emma, we'll need to do better," Reagan says. "I'd like to propose a homework assignment." Everyone groans.

"Now, now, give Reagan a chance. What do you have in mind?" Mr. Burnett asks.

"I think we need a rubric for the jokes we send Emma. Like one of the rubrics you make for our projects. If laughter is the best medicine, then we need jokes and riddles that will actually make Emma laugh." Reagan has come up with an interesting idea. I could have used a rubric for my dad's knock-knock joke the other night.

"I like it!" Mr. Burnett says. "I'll give you people two nights to work on a joke rubric. Let's see, how about at least three categories. And please include *funny* as the most important category. Now, let's get back to last night's geometry assignment. But before we do, I have one more question. Are you ready?"

When Mr. Burnett asks the class if we're ready, we're all supposed to respond together, and we do: "READY!" We practically shout the word.

"How do you keep warm in a cold room?" Mr. Burnett asks. Oh no, I don't think I can handle another one of Mr. Burnett's so-called jokes. Matthew calls out again.

"Wear a sweater," he says.

"Well, you could wear a sweater, Matthew. Or, you could stand in the corner where it's always ninety degrees." Mr. Burnett is so proud of his geometry joke. We reward him with loud groans.

But the truth is, I think we love our teacher even more. Although he's earned a Needs Improvement in the funny category, he always gets Exceptional for effort.

Chapter 35
Chester's Training

My dad was right. His hospital has a training program for pet therapy teams. I soon learn the program is going to be a lot more difficult than I expected. From what I've read, this training would *Exceed Expectations* on a rigor rubric.

For one thing, there will be a huge test at the end of the training. Like most kids, I'm not a fan of tests, but this one doesn't sound fair. Chester and I need to pass ten subtests before the final exam. And each subtest includes so many "automatic failures" I'm panicking. I guess I expected something like a rubric, not this old-fashioned pass-fail system.

For example, if a dog growls, or acts shy, or eats a treat he's not supposed to eat, or even pulls on his leash during a subtest—it's an automatic failure. Mr. Burnett would have a rubric for temperament, grooming, following directions, friendliness. In his classroom, everyone would have opportunities to improve. But not for pet therapy school. No second chances, no do-overs. Pass this test or it's out the door.

It's a Thursday night, the first night of training, and I'm sitting between my mom and dad in a large room in the basement of the hospital. Chester's leaning against my leg, and I can feel him quivering. Even my parents seem nervous as we wait in a large circle with the other human-canine teams.

The dogs in the room come in all shapes, sizes, breeds, and temperaments. Across from us, there's a Yorkshire terrier who acts like it's playtime at the dog park. That Yorkie can't stop yapping and bothering the other trainees. Next to us is a dopey-looking beagle mix, who's farting every twenty seconds. Between the Yorkie and the beagle, I'm not worried about Chester's competition.

I soon realize we'll have to practice a ton at home. "There will be homework, Chester," I whisper loud enough for my parents to hear. I want them to know I'm serious about this. Once Chester and I are trained, we can visit Emma every day, all summer long. Together we'll increase her odds of beating cancer. And it's wonderful to be doing something as a family again. Mom, Dad, Chester, and me. Finally, a happy family of four, which was the one thing I've been wishing for all these years.

On the way home, Dad insists we stop for ice cream. Maybe he's looking for an excuse to keep our family together for a little longer. I'm proud of Chester for not trying to lick my cone. I'm thinking he's going to ace this training. He's already doing well in the self-control category. When we pull up outside our house, Dad surprises me again.

"Let's all go inside, finish our ice cream cones, and talk for a while," he says. "I don't have to be back at the ER for another hour." This is an excellent sign. Not only did my parents not argue about anything in the car or during the training, but now my dad wants to hang out with us. With all of us—Chester, my mom, and me.

Chester curls up in his dog bed on the living room floor, and my parents sit next to each other on the couch. I'm on the floor in front of the coffee table, so I can pet Chester. We're enjoying our ice cream, excited about the training, feeling good about helping Emma.

And then my mom has to go and ruin everything. "Georgia, Dad and I want to talk to you about our plans." Her voice cracks, and my heart sinks like a broken old rowboat filled with water. I stop eating. My hands start to tremble. Thankfully, the ice cream cone has one of those flat bottoms, and I put it on the coffee table so I don't drop the darn thing. I start braiding my hair with my sticky fingers. I need to focus on what my mom is saying, but I'm too afraid to look at her. I stare at my dad's face instead. He's gazing down at the floor.

"Your plans? What do you mean 'your plans?'" I ask. I want to throw something, scream at someone, smash something. I want to put my hands over my ears like a three-year-old. But I hold all my feelings inside, and I wait.

"Honey, your mom and I have agreed this is not going to work out for us. We both love you so much. We don't want to hurt you, but we've decided we can't live together anymore." I can't remember ever seeing my dad cry, and the tears spilling down his face terrify me. He doesn't sob or make any noise at all. But he wipes his cheeks with the back of his hand.

"Georgia, your dad is trying to say we've decided to get a divorce. But we want you to know, we're not going to fight anymore. We're not going to fight about anything. We promise you," my mom says.

"I don't care if you fight. Everyone fights," I snap. "You can fight every day if you want to, but please, don't get a divorce!" What's left of my ice cream cone is oozing all over the coffee table.

"Georgia, this is hard for us, too," my dad says. That's a ridiculous thing for any parent to say. Everyone knows divorce is hardest on the kids. Why do *my* parents have to be part of the 46.6 percent? I mean, the odds weren't great, but they were in our favor.

"Then don't get a divorce! Stay married. You don't have to do this!" I'm whining, I'm pleading, but I can't stop myself. My mom grabs my melting ice cream cone. She wipes the coffee table with a napkin and walks into the kitchen. She can't stand a mess anywhere, so why is she making a mess of my life?

While Mom's in the kitchen, I look up at my dad, and I plead. "Please, don't do this. You don't have to get a divorce. You can try to work things out. Please, Dad." My mom returns, and she sits on the floor, on the other side of Chester.

Her voice is soft and low, but I feel every word like a punch to my gut. "Georgia, this is something we're going to do. We're going to get a divorce. This decision was hard for us. But it has nothing to do with you or how much we love you," she says. "You know that, right?" Now she's the one pleading. I can't give either one of them what they want. There will be no permission from me. What do they expect me to say? *Sure guys, that's fine. Break up this family. I don't care. Hey, I'll get two Christmases and an extra birthday party every year. This is a good thing! Thank you!*

"Come on, Chester," I say. I stand up, take a few steps toward my bedroom, and turn around. "You've made your decision, and there's nothing I can say or do to change anything. I'm going to bed." And I walk away, Chester at my heels. I don't yell. I don't scream. I don't throw anything. I pretend I can handle this, that I can handle anything. I fake it until I shut my bedroom door behind me, and then I double over.

Chester jumps on my lap. I cry a bucket of tears into his soft fur, and he gets to practice comforting someone who is in terrible pain. This wasn't the homework I planned for Chester, but he does his best trying to numb the throbbing ache in my heart.

Chapter 36
More Knock-Knock Jokes

Only a few more weeks of sixth grade. This will be the first summer our family won't be vacationing together. My dad is taking me to the Cape for a week in July—just the two of us. In August, my mom, Aunt Felicia, Sam, and I are going to spend a week in New York City. We rented an apartment with two bedrooms, and we're going to get tickets for Broadway shows, visit museums, go to Ellis Island, and do all the touristy things people do when they visit the city. Even though I'm excited about both vacations, I'd give up my whole summer and all those plans to have my family back together.

Chester doesn't get a summer vacation, but he definitely deserves one. He aced all of his exams, and the pet therapy trainers even gave him a special award for being the kindest canine in the class. I'm hanging his award on the refrigerator next to my report card from last term.

It's weird how great my parents are getting along now they've decided to end their marriage. My mom says she's still hurting. She's lonely, but she tells me she's not ready to date other men, thank goodness. And my dad says he and Erin are still friends, nothing more. I've decided my parents' love lives are none of my business.

Chester and I are ready for our first volunteer assignment as a certified pet therapy team. We're going to the pediatric oncology ward to visit the youngest cancer patients. Emma is still in Baltimore finishing up her treatment. But until my best friend comes home, Chester will do his magic for the children who are fighting cancer at my dad's hospital. Magic that has nothing to do with a Magic 8 Ball.

"Listen, Georgia," my dad says when he calls me the night before our first pet therapy assignment. "I want you to be prepared for this."

"Dad, Chester and I are totally prepared. We aced the training. Remember? You were there!"

"I'm not worried about Chester; it's you I'm worried about."

"Gee, thanks, Dad. Thanks for your vote of confidence."

"That's not what I meant. You know I have confidence in you. This has nothing to do with your abilities, your skills, or your knowledge. It's upsetting for anyone the first time they visit these young patients."

"Dad, I know what to expect. Kids fighting cancer. I get it."

"Some of the children you'll meet are very, very sick, Georgia."

"Dad, I know they're sick. That's the whole point. Chester and I are going there to help them get better."

"Okay. I don't want you to be surprised."

"I won't, Dad. Trust me for once in your life."

Before we leave for the hospital, I put Chester's front legs through the openings in his new red vest. The blue embroidered letters read, CHESTER – Certified Pet Therapy Animal. My matching vest says Pet Therapy Handler.

I'm so proud of that dog I take a zillion pictures of him from all different angles and distances. I like the close-up shots best, but I need to step back to get the full effect of his vest. I'm turning into my corny mother, who insists on taking pictures of me each year on my first and last days of school.

When we reach the hospital, my mom parks in the visitors' lot. I feel everyone's eyes on Chester as we walk through the front entrance. People are checking him out and smiling as we make our way toward the elevator. We're waiting outside the volunteer coordinator's office, when a woman asks, "May I pet your dog?" She's sitting in a wheelchair, hooked up to a pole with tubes connecting her to some medicine that's dripping into a vein on her arm.

"Of course," I say. I watch as Chester does his magic. The woman smiles and crinkles her eyes as she gently pets Chester's head.

The volunteer coordinator's name is Margot. Chester isn't the only dog volunteering, but he's happy to share the spotlight with two golden retrievers and a smaller dog named Trixie. Trixie looks like she's a mix of ten different breeds. She has a little pink bow in her hair. Chester seems to like her. I have to remind him twice to stop sniffing his new friend.

Margot checks in with each team, making sure the dogs are well-groomed and their handlers are in control of their pets. She assigns each team a block of hospital rooms on the floor. "I can't tell you what a difference you all make," Margot says. "Our patients and our medical team look forward to your visits every week. They are so excited to see you. Go spread some joy, everyone." And like that, we're off, heading toward the pediatric oncology ward, eager to spread some joy.

We enter room 302. A little girl is sitting up, looking so tiny in her large hospital bed, so lost and alone. A woman, who must be her mom, is sitting in a chair next to her, and the doctor is trying to listen to the girl's lungs with a stethoscope. The little girl is squirming, pushing the doctor's hands away. I remember acting like that when I was little. Kids don't like to be poked.

"Oh look, Charlotte, you have a visitor!" her mom says. Charlotte stops squirming. I watch as her face transforms from fear of the doctor and the stethoscope to pure happiness to see Chester.

"I'm Georgia, and this is Chester," I say, walking into the room. "You must be Charlotte." My mom stays near the door, letting Chester and me do our thing.

"Can Chester sit on my bed?" Charlotte asks. Her mom looks up at the doctor who nods yes. Gently, I place Chester at the foot of the bed. He knows what to do. He walks over and stretches out next to the little girl's side. Charlotte rubs Chester's head, behind his ears, talking to him the whole time. "It's okay, Chester. Everything is going to be fine. Don't worry, Chester," she says. Then the doctor tilts her head at me, her eyes sparkling.

"Do you think we could listen to Chester's breathing with this stethoscope?" she asks me.

"I don't think Chester would mind," I say. "Let's give it a try." Chester is so obedient. He rolls over on command and waits patiently as the doctor presses the metal disk at the end of her stethoscope to his chest, listening to his lungs breathing and his heart beating. The whole time, Chester is gazing up into

Charlotte's eyes as if he's saying, "It's not too bad. You can do this."

"Charlotte, would you like to listen to Chester's heart?" the doctor asks. Charlotte is beaming. The doctor puts the earpieces in Charlotte's ears. She listens to Chester's heart beating strong, and with the doctor's guidance, she moves the stethoscope gently across his chest.

"Mommy, Chester's so brave," she says. "I can be brave, too." Now it's Chester's turn to watch as the doctor listens to Charlotte's heart and lungs.

My mom reminds me we have other patients to visit. I hate to leave this perfect moment. As I turn to leave, I'm not sad about my parents' marriage, I'm not worrying about Emma, I'm not thinking about my uncle's business, or what happened yesterday, or what might happen tomorrow. I'm here, with Chester and Charlotte, and it's where I want to be. I promise Charlotte we'll be back in a week.

Our next visit is with a little boy. His head is wrapped in thick white bandages, and he's wearing a Red Sox cap. A nurse walks over to welcome us. She wants to pet Chester and love him up a little before she has to share him with her patient.

"Timmy, your visitor is here," the nurse says. She turns to us and whispers, "Timmy's not having a great day. But let's see if he's up for a short visit with... let me see, the name on his vest says... it's Chester. What a cutie you are, Chester!" He wags his tail. That dog is a sucker for compliments. We follow the nurse into the darkened room.

"Hi, Timmy, this is Chester. I'm Georgia," I say. Timmy lifts his little hand and waves to us. I see a flicker of a smile appear, and then it disappears, like the blink of an eye.

"Timmy, would you like to pet Chester?" the nurse asks. He nods his head. I place Chester on the bed. He puts his sweet face on Timmy's leg and looks up at him with so much love, my heart is practically bursting with pride.

"How old is he?" Timmy asks.

"I think he's five or six. We adopted him from the Humane Society. They weren't sure how old he was when we first met him."

"I'm adopted, too," Timmy says. "I was a baby."

"Really? We're lucky we adopted Chester, and your parents are lucky they adopted you."

"Yeah, I know," Timmy says. "Can he do tricks?" I think about the Magic 8 Ball. Was that some kind of trick? Was it magic? Or was it all about chance and probability?

"Not really. No tricks, but Chester's a good listener, and he understands a lot. And you know what, Timmy? Chester always makes me feel better, no matter how sad I am. I guess that's a kind of trick, right?"

Timmy laughs, and then he says, "Want to hear a joke?"

Timmy and I spend the next ten minutes sharing silly knock-knock jokes. For some weird reason, I find them funny, and I don't need a rubric to judge them. Unlike my dad and my math teacher, Timmy might actually have a future as a stand-up comic.

Chapter 37
Emma's Back!

Hard to believe it's already the last week of school. All the kids and most teachers are counting down the days. But not Mr. Burnett. He acts like it's the first week of school, as if it's some badge of honor for him to fill every single day with as much math as he can stuff into our brains. No end-of-year celebrations. No wasting time with movies, taking down bulletin board displays, or cleaning the classroom. Just math, math, and more math.

Today he seems more excited than usual, and it's not about math for a change. He's practically jumping up and down, giving everyone high fives at the door.

"Folks, I have some news." He has our full attention. "Emma has sent our class a thank-you note for all the jokes and get-well cards. She *loved* the music video we made. Especially the part where Matthew dances and lip-syncs to the Taylor Swift song about being strong and fighting back."

"Woo-hoo!" Matthew jumps up and starts breakdancing. Everyone laughs, and Mr. Burnett can't get annoyed because he's in such a good mood.

"Emma's parents sent us a thank-you note, too. And… her mom dropped off a plate of these homemade brownies for us!" He's holding a plate in one hand, and with the other hand he removes a cloth napkin like he's a magician revealing a rabbit. We start to clap, and that gives Matthew another excuse to dance. "Okay, everyone. Settle down, settle down." Beth passes around the plate of brownies. While she's doing that, Mr. Burnett reads the thank-you notes aloud.

Turns out my idea helped Emma a ton. Her parents say she loved our jokes. Reagan's idea was a big hit, too. Emma watches the music video almost every day, and she thinks all the laughter has helped her fight the disease. Reagan looks over at me when Mr. Burnett reads the letter. She smiles and gives me a thumbs up. I smile back. We both had great ideas, and it turns out we were an amazing team.

But here's the real reason Mr. Burnett is so happy and excited. He tells us Emma's leukemia is in remission. And this time he doesn't stop us from applauding, yelling, and jumping out of our seats.

We made two hundred and forty-eight dollars at the bake sale, which doesn't go very far in the world of cancer research. But Mr. Burnett says every dollar counts. Then, because he can't help himself, he makes us estimate how much money kids could raise for cancer research if every middle school in America had a bake sale that did as well as our bake sale. He can't stop himself from turning everything into a math problem. I feel sorry for his wife and children.

Even though Emma's back home from Baltimore, she isn't ready to return to school for this last week. Everyone's optimistic she'll be strong enough by the beginning of a new school year.

That night, I write a note to Emma's parents, thanking them for the brownies. I tell them about Chester's pet therapy training and about our volunteer visits to the pediatric ward at the hospital. I ask them if Chester and I can visit Emma.

Her mom calls a few days later. She'll check with Emma's doctor, but she knows Emma would love to see me. "Georgia, I have to tell you, Emma loved your cards and your letters most of all. She told us all about your pet therapy training. We're so proud of you, and we can't wait to see you and Chester."

A few weeks later, I'm well into my summer vacation mindset. I've packed my suitcase for the Cape, and I'm ready to leave the next day. But today I have bigger plans.

Chester hops into the back seat of our car. I sit in the front with my mom, guarding the plate of chocolate chip cookies we baked for Emma and her family. Chester is extremely obedient, but no dog can be trusted with chocolate chip cookies.

"Honey, are you nervous?" my mom asks.

"No. Why would you say that?"

"You're tapping your foot. And you're braiding and unbraiding your hair."

"I always tap my foot and braid my hair. It doesn't mean I'm nervous." Geez. My mom notices everything. I decide to tell her the truth.

"I don't know what to expect. I'm afraid of how Emma might have changed," I say.

"She's been through a lot. But you and Chester will do fine. You've done a terrific job at the hospital with the young oncology patients."

"Chester's always fine. I'm not worried about him." I turn around and look in the backseat to check on Chester. He lifts his head as if to say, *Yup. I'm fine. Don't worry about me.* "And it's different at the hospital, Mom. When I'm with those kids, I forget they're sick."

We pull up to the front of Emma's house. My mom takes the plate of cookies from my hands. I clip Chester's leash onto his collar. I gave him a bath last night and brushed his coat. He smells like lilacs, and he looks especially handsome today.

I take a deep breath. I try to focus on why I'm here. *I'm here to help Emma with her recovery. I'm here because, although I know there are plenty of things in my life I can't control, there are some things I can control. I'm here because, like all those messages in a Magic 8 Ball, sometimes the answers in life are hazy, unpredictable, improbable, and disappointing. But other times, like today, everything points to a positive outlook, a likely YES. I'm learning to improve the odds, and I don't need a Magic 8 Ball.*

I look down at Chester. He's ready to do some magic of his own. Or is he? And that's when I understand another layer of truth about why we're here, standing outside Emma's door.

It's not about magic or probability. It's not about the past or the future. It's not even about improving the odds. Chester's here because he likes being with me. He's enjoying the moment, as always. That's Chester. And me? I want to see Emma. She's my best friend. I've missed her so much, and I like hanging out with her. That's why I'm here, and that's reason enough.

The End

Acknowledgements

I am fortunate to have a team of family and friends who helped me bring *Chester and the Magic 8 Ball* into the world:

My daughter, Johanna Katz, who convinced me to visit the Humane Society "just to look." I'll never forget the day when a toothless rescue dog jumped into our hearts, filling our lives with even more love. *Without a doubt.*

My editor and niece, Samantha Holtgrewe, the coolest comma-queen of all time. *It is certain.*

My brother-in-law, Doug Holtgrewe, whose magnificent mugs and bowls have a place in my cupboards and now a place in this novel. *It is decidedly so.*

My sister and first reader, Phyllis Holtgrewe, for never failing to encourage me. I can always *count on it.*

My daughter-in-law, Siwei Liao Katz, for the "goldfish test" story and for giving us a future reader for my middle-grade novels. *My sources say YES!*

My brilliant critique partners, Beth Brody, Kelly Kandra Hugh, and Pam Kelly, who have never given up on Chester. *All signs point to Yes!*

My dear friends, Susan Seider and Peppy, an inspirational pet therapy team. *You may rely on it.*

My publisher and his fearless team, Reagan Rothe, David King, Justin Weeks, and Christopher Miller, for giving my story a forever home. *Outlook good.*

My sister, Martha Plaine, and my good friend, Larry Paterno, who helped me grapple with my math phobia and embrace the challenge. The key was always *concentrate and try again.*

And always, always, always, Robert Katz, my husband and best friend. I never need to *ask again later* and the reply is never *hazy.* I am so incredibly lucky.

About The Author

Lynn Katz is a former teacher, curriculum writer, and school principal with a soft spot in her heart for toothless, rescue dogs. A full time fiction writer, her debut novel, *The Surrogate*, was published in May 2021. Lynn Katz lives in Connecticut. When not reading or writing, Lynn can be found hiking or kayaking with her husband.

Note From the Author

Word-of-mouth is crucial for any author to succeed. If you enjoyed *Chester and the Magic 8 Ball*, please leave a review online—anywhere you are able. Even if it's just a sentence or two. It would make all the difference and would be very much appreciated.

Thanks!
Lynn Katz

We hope you enjoyed reading this title from:

BLACK ROSE writing™

CPSIA information can be obtained
at www.ICGtesting.com
Printed in the USA
LVHW031700250523
748062LV00002B/235